Books in the American Dog series:

Poppy
Chestnut
Star

D0064169

AMERICAN DOG
★ BRAVE ★

BY JENNIFER LI SHOTZ

HOUGHTON MIFFLIN HARCOURT
BOSTON   NEW YORK

Copyright © 2020 by Alloy Entertainment

All rights reserved. For information about permission to reproduce selections from this book,
write to trade.permissions@hmhco.com or to Permissions, Houghton Mifflin Harcourt
Publishing Company, 3 Park Avenue, 19th Floor, New York, New York 10016.

hmhbooks.com

Produced by Alloy Entertainment

alloy**entertainment**

30 Hudson Yards
New York, NY 10001

The text was set in Adobe Caslon Pro.

Library of Congress Cataloging in Publication Data
Names: Shotz, Jennifer Li, author.
Title: Brave / by Jennifer Li Shotz.
Description: Boston ; New York : Houghton Mifflin Harcourt, [2020] |
Series: American dog | Audience: Ages 7 to 10. | Audience: Grades 2–3. |
Summary: When twelve-year-old Dylan rescues Brave, he knows it will take
hard work, patience, and training to convince his parents that he can
keep the skittish stray dog.
Identifiers: LCCN 2019045790 (print) | LCCN 2019045791 (ebook) |
ISBN 9780358108726 (trade paperback) | ISBN
9780358108610 (ebook) | ISBN 9780358343080 (ebook) | ISBN 9780358343219
(ebook)
Subjects: CYAC: Dogs—Fiction. | Friendship—Fiction. | Family
life—Texas—Fiction. | San Antonio (Tex.)—Fiction.
Classification: LCC PZ7.1.S51784 Br 2020 (print) | LCC PZ7.1.S51784
(ebook) | DDC [Fic]—dc23
LC record available at https://lccn.loc.gov/2019045790
LC ebook record available at https://lccn.loc.gov/2019045791

ISBN: 978-0-358-10867-2 paper over board
ISBN: 978-0-358-10872-6 paperback

Manufactured in the United States of America
DOC 10 9 8 7 6 5 4 3 2 1
4500792933

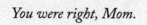

You were right, Mom.

★ CHAPTER 1 ★

"How about these?" Dylan held out a plastic packet of multicolored water balloons.

Jaxon, his best friend since forever, took the pack from Dylan's hand and held it up for inspection. "Perfect," he declared. "Just the right size for a good soaking."

The boys were gearing up for their last epic water balloon fight of the season. School had started for the year, but it was still hot enough in Texas for a full-scale battle—and Dylan and Jaxon were an unstoppable team. Their signature move was to ambush their friends from two sides at once—and they'd never lost. Not once.

Jaxon tossed the package back to Dylan, who caught it in midair.

Dylan grabbed four more water balloon packs from the rack and headed for the register.

"When are we doing this?" Dylan asked. "Tomorrow?"

"If you can handle it!" Jaxon punched him on the shoulder and Dylan winced.

"You're going to regret that!" Dylan chased Jaxon to the front of the store, where the cashier eyed them sternly.

The boys slowed to a walk. Dylan cleared his throat and dumped a handful of change on the counter. Jaxon's long brown hair flopped into his eyes as he looked down and turned his jeans pockets inside out to grab every last coin. Together they had just enough, even if Dylan was contributing more of his allowance than Jaxon was.

"I'll take those." Dylan grabbed the shopping bag from Jaxon as they walked out of the store. He hopped on his bike, ready to head for home. "I'll text you later to make a plan of attack. I have some ideas for a new strategy."

"Hey, Dyl, actually, I had an idea too." Jaxon rubbed his chin thoughtfully, like he had thought of something brilliant. "What if we ditch the fight and do something else entirely?"

Dylan shot Jaxon a skeptical look, to be sure his friend wasn't just messing with him. The showdown was tradition. Why wouldn't Jaxon want to play—or win—anymore? "What are you talking about?" Dylan asked doubtfully.

"I'm just saying, maybe now that we're in sixth grade, having a water balloon fight every weekend is for little kids." Jaxon shrugged like it was no big deal.

Dylan couldn't believe it—Jaxon was serious. "I mean . . . I guess, maybe?" Dylan tried not to sound disappointed. If Jaxon suddenly thought the whole thing was babyish, he didn't want to admit that he was looking forward to it.

Since kindergarten, Dylan and Jaxon had always been like two sides of the same coin. They had played on the same soccer teams and gone to the same swimming classes. They had even looked alike until recently, when Dylan had his dark brown hair buzzed down to the usual crew cut to match his dad's military cut, while Jaxon had let his hair grow out.

But Dylan had to admit that it wasn't just their hair that had changed recently. Dylan had also noticed that at school, the other guys had started to treat Jaxon a little differently. It was like he and Jaxon and their friends had always been a pack—equals—but now Jaxon had moved to the front of it, and the guys would do anything he told them to. Dylan had started to feel less like Jaxon's friend and more like his follower. It seemed to Dylan that Jaxon had noticed it too— and kind of liked it.

"Come on, Dyl—don't you ever get . . . I don't know . . . tired of doing the same stuff all the time?"

The question took Dylan by surprise. "Uh . . . no. I mean, sometimes?" He felt something squirm in his stomach— like somehow Jaxon was reading his mind. He did get tired of some stuff, but not the water balloon fights. "I just think we should do something *really* different this time," Jaxon said. "We're twelve. Maybe we should do something . . . I don't know . . . cooler."

Jaxon's words stung, but Dylan did his best not to let it show. He couldn't say Jaxon's suggestion was coming out of nowhere. With his new status, Jaxon had been pushing boundaries lately, as Dylan's mom would call it—asking Dylan to stay out late, skipping his homework, and thinking up elaborate pranks. Dylan liked having fun, and Jaxon always acted like whatever he had in mind was going to be the *most* fun thing ever. And if Dylan or one of the other guys hesitated, Jaxon was quick to tease them in front of everyone else.

So Dylan had been telling himself to just go along with whatever Jaxon suggested, even when he wasn't so sure it was such a good idea. *What's the worst that can happen?* he'd recently found himself wondering more often than he'd care to admit.

"Like what?" Dylan asked, trying to sound cool himself.

Jaxon shrugged and jumped onto his bike. "Let me think . . ." A strange look crossed his face that Dylan had never seen before. There was a glint in his eye and a smirk on his lips—and it made Dylan instantly uncomfortable.

"Um, why are you looking at me like that?" Dylan asked, not entirely sure he wanted to know the answer.

"You know that video I sent you? Of the guy with the hose?"

Dylan nodded, hoping Jaxon wouldn't notice that he was just playing along. He didn't remember that video because he hadn't watched it—or most of the others Jaxon and their other friends had sent in the last few days. He'd meant to, and even held his finger above the play arrow a couple of times. But he just hadn't done it. Lately, while Jaxon and their other friends were high-fiving and fist-bumping and *hey-bro*-ing about things Dylan usually cared about, he found himself tuning out. What so-and-so posted on Instagram. The latest Nintendo news. A viral YouTube video. Sometimes Dylan thought it just seemed . . . boring.

"Yeah, sure. That one was crazy," Dylan said.

Jaxon broke out into a full grin. "So what if we copied that video, but instead of using a hose, we throw water balloons at the cars?"

This time, Dylan's stomach did a full churning somersault. "You want to throw water balloons . . . at cars? Isn't that . . . I mean, that's not . . . Is that a good idea?"

Jaxon's eyes bulged out of his head. "A good idea? It's a great idea!"

Dylan just stared back at him, unsure what to say. It was a terrible idea—a dangerous idea. This time, Jaxon was going too far.

"Come on, Dyl—I thought you'd be up for a little adventure." Jaxon mouthed *boom!* and mimed a water balloon exploding with his hands. He was getting excited now.

Dylan was quiet as he thought it over. He didn't want to say yes, but he really didn't know how to say no.

"Dude!" Jaxon laughed. "What is going on with you? What have you done with my best friend?"

"Nothing!" Dylan forced himself to smile.

"Good. Because I don't want to tell anyone else until after we do it. It'll be so much crazier if we surprise the guys with our own video."

Something about the look in Jaxon's eye told Dylan that he wasn't going to take no for an answer, even if Dylan tried to get out of it.

"Tomorrow. We're doing this," Jaxon said.

"Okay, fine, we're doing this."

Before Jaxon could question his enthusiasm, Dylan's phone buzzed in his back pocket. Secretly relieved at the interruption, he checked the alert reminding him to get home. He had promised his mom he'd do his chores and get a head start on his homework, but if he didn't leave soon, he was going to be late.

"I . . . um . . . I'll see you tomorrow," Dylan said.

Jaxon zoomed past Dylan with a cackle and grabbed the bag of water balloons out of his hand. "It's gonna be awesome, Dyl!" he shouted over his shoulder, now in the lead.

"Yeah," Dylan muttered to himself, pedaling slowly after his friend. "Awesome. Right."

★ CHAPTER 2 ★

The wind whipped against Dylan's face as he raced his bike down the street. He'd left Jaxon at the turnoff to his street and had to hurry home if he had any hope of beating his mom. He swerved around a tree branch lying at an angle in the road—a remnant of the hurricane that had pounded the city a couple of weeks earlier.

Not that Dylan needed any reminders. The memory of the hurricane was burned into his brain forever: the wind as loud as a speeding train, trees snapping like twigs and slamming into buildings, windows exploding like they'd been dynamited. It had been a terrifying few hours. He and his mom had spent the entire night lying awake in their bathtub, listening to the destruction outside and hoping the walls around them would withstand the force of the storm.

The city had hauled away most of the big wreckage, but there were still pockets of splintered plywood and wet debris scattered on the streets. The shock from the storm lingered along with the mess, but people had jumped into action to try to help one another through it. Neighbors had banded together to carry bucket after bucket of water from flooded living rooms. They had cleaned up yards and hammered boards over the gaping holes in the sides of their houses. People from the block had been especially helpful to Dylan and his mom because his dad was a soldier deployed in the Middle East.

Countless families had been forced to move out of their mangled homes, and it seemed like a lot of them might not ever come back. Dylan knew he and his mom had been lucky. Except for a few patches of roof that had been sheared right off, and a giant hole in the exterior wall by the front door, their house had fared pretty well.

Dylan sped up, swerving toward the sidewalk when he saw that the street ahead was clogged with traffic. He scooted back on the seat, shifting his weight until he was about to tip over, then yanked up on the handlebars at just the right second. He popped a half wheelie over the curb and whizzed by a woman carrying a bag of groceries to her car.

"Hey!" she yelled.

"Sorry!" Dylan shouted behind him. He kept going, reminding himself to slow down around pedestrians.

As Dylan made his way down the street, a delicious smell wafted toward him. He would know that scent anywhere: Tio Suerte tacos, voted best tacos in San Antonio three years running. They'd been closed since the hurricane, and Dylan's stomach rumbled at the thought of them finally being reopened. He could practically taste the beef taco already.

One little detour couldn't hurt.

He pulled a hard left and slammed on his handlebar brakes, skidding to a stop on the loose gravel in the Tio Suerte parking lot. Just as he dropped his bike to the ground, Dylan heard a man shout in the alley behind the restaurant.

"Get out of here, you dirty little rat!"

Dylan stuck his head around the side of the building and peeked down the alley. An old man in an apron waved a fist in the air—but it wasn't a rat he was chasing—it was a dirty gray dog. The cook stomped his foot on the asphalt, and the dog whimpered and scuttled backwards into the corner by the dumpster, his ears back and down and his tail tucked between his legs. The chef was angry—really angry—and Dylan could tell that the dog was scared.

The cook grabbed a broom and whacked the handle hard against the side of the metal dumpster, which let out a terrifying rumble. The dog flinched at the loud noise. The man was trying to scare the dog away, but the pup was so petrified that it was having the opposite effect.

"Get out of here!" the cook shouted. "*¡Lágate!*"

The dog hunkered down, shaking. Dylan had recently seen a few other strays wandering the city. He wondered if there were more of them because of the hurricane. But there was something about this dog that caught Dylan's eye—it seemed so scared and sad. Did this pup have a family?

Dylan suddenly felt protective of the poor dog, who had probably just been following the mouth-watering aroma of the tacos, like he had.

"I think he's hungry," Dylan called to the cook.

The man shot him an irritated look. "Every day he's hungry. The little monster won't leave."

Dylan studied the animal more closely. The dog looked from him to the cook and back again with big, round, frightened eyes—eyes that were a surprisingly intense amber color. There was no way this dog had a home, Dylan thought. His ribs were showing under his fur, and he was filthy—his coat was matted and stiff. He wasn't wearing a collar or tags. And why would he stick around an alley getting yelled at if he had somewhere else to be? He had to be a stray.

"How long has he been hanging around?" Dylan asked, getting closer.

"He's been here for at least a week," the chef replied. "I've called animal control a hundred times, but this dog is too fast. They can't catch him." As the cook spoke, he took a step forward and tried to grab the dog. But the pup really was quick—he disappeared under the dumpster as the cook's fingers snatched at nothing but air.

The cook waved the broom handle one last time, then went inside, slamming the kitchen door behind him.

The second the man was gone, the dog popped his nose out and sniffed at the air, then scanned the alley. When he saw that the coast was clear, he crept out from under the dumpster and looked up at Dylan.

"You okay, boy?" Dylan asked, speaking softly. He didn't want to scare the dog more.

The dog gave a nervous wag of his tail and gazed at Dylan with a sweet but desperate look in his eye.

Dylan and the dog stared at each other while Dylan's mind buzzed.

Clearly this dog was starving. He couldn't just leave it here, could he? That's not the type of thing his parents had raised him to do—to leave someone in trouble. And this dog was definitely in trouble.

Maybe—just maybe—if he took the dog home and fed it and gave it a good hot bath . . . his parents would let him keep it. After all, Dylan had been begging his parents for a dog for a long time. They'd said no a thousand different ways, but the last time he'd asked, his mom hadn't actually said *no*. She'd pursed her lips and said *We'll see*, which was a subtle upgrade that gave Dylan a tiny bit of hope. Maybe meeting the right dog would finally convince her. And this stray guy, with his striking eyes and funny tail wag, seemed like the right dog. Dylan couldn't explain it, but it felt like he and the dog already knew each other somehow, as if they were already bonded.

And even if his mom was mad at first, Dylan knew it wouldn't be the end of the world. Jaxon always said it was better to ask for forgiveness than permission. Since asking for a dog hadn't worked too well, maybe if he just brought one home and apologized a lot, his parents would let him keep it. Besides, how could they say no to a sad, hungry stray that didn't have a family?

Dylan made up his mind right then and there: The dog was coming home with him.

He took a step toward the dog, who eyed him warily but stood still. Dylan took another step. When he got closer, he could see that underneath the layer of grime, the animal's coat wasn't quite gray—it was a mix of dark gray and blue that Dylan had never seen before. The dog was on the small-ish side, but he was thick with muscle, his short legs powerful. The dog's ears pointed straight up, ending in sharp points that framed his head. Dylan thought about a small dog like this surviving on the streets, fending for himself while people like the cook shouted and chased him away.

The dog would have to be very brave to have survived so long on his own.

"Come here, buddy," Dylan said softly. He held out a hand for the dog to sniff, but he took a few scuttling steps backwards, huddling in the corner by the dumpster again.

"Sorry—I didn't mean to scare you," Dylan said. He backed away a couple of steps.

With a little distance between them, the dog seemed to calm down. His ears dropped as he cocked his head to the side and watched Dylan carefully. Since he didn't have a collar or tags, there was no way for Dylan to know his name —if he even had one.

"How about I call you Brave?" Dylan said. "Because that's what you must be if you're surviving out here on your own."

Brave wagged his tail once. Dylan took that as a good sign.

"Sit, Brave."

Brave blinked and furrowed his brow a little, as if he were thinking hard about Dylan's command. Dylan waited for the dog to sit, but he didn't. Brave just watched him expectantly, his eyes bright and his ears perked up.

Though he was dirty and a little scared, there was

something very calm about Brave. He was definitely a good dog—how had he ended up hungry and on the streets? That didn't seem fair to Dylan. Not one bit.

He had an idea.

"Stay here," Dylan said to Brave. Then he disappeared around the side of the building and came back pushing his bike and hopping on it at the same time.

"Follow me, okay?" he said to Brave. "I mean, come."

Dylan rode slowly out of the parking lot, giving the dog time to catch up. At first Brave watched him ride away, and Dylan wasn't sure his plan would work. After a moment, the dog stood up and took a few tentative steps after the bike —then hesitated and sat back down. It was almost as if he wasn't sure if he should follow Dylan but he didn't want to be left alone.

Dylan coasted at a crawl, looking back over his shoulder. Brave took a few more steps and began to follow him, trailing a safe distance behind. Dylan pedaled and picked up a little speed.

About a block from the restaurant, Dylan spotted a dark blur by his right leg. He looked down.

It was Brave. The dog was running right next to him. Dylan sped up, and Brave picked up the pace too.

"Man, you're fast!"

Soon Dylan was pumping his legs as fast as he could,

and Brave raced beside him with ease. He even looked like he was enjoying himself. His gait was smooth, his tail was pointed up to the sky, and his tongue dangled from his mouth in what almost looked like a lazy smile.

Dylan pedaled, Brave ran, and together they made it all the way home.

★ CHAPTER 3 ★

Dylan's family lived on Juniper Hill Road on the northwest edge of San Antonio, where the city gave way to country-side beyond. Dylan's house was on a residential street with a paved road, but just a few homes away from his, the street intersected with a county road that led straight to ranch land. It was city on one side and country on the other, two different worlds colliding. Depending on which way the wind was blowing, you could smell either the horses or the cows from the Garcia Ranch, just a half mile down the road. If you were unlucky, sometimes you could smell both at the same time.

Dylan rode straight into the open garage, Brave at his heels. He hopped off the bike and turned around to find Brave sniffing at a pile of his dad's fishing gear. The rods and reels and tackle boxes stuffed with lures and spindles of translucent line took up a quarter of the garage—and always made Dylan's mom roll her eyes.

"Don't touch Dad's stuff!" he warned Brave. The dog flinched at the sound of Dylan's voice. "Sorry, buddy," Dylan said, lowering his voice. "I didn't mean to scare you." Brave's body relaxed a little. "It's just that the fishing gear is off-limits—it's Dad's favorite thing in the whole world," Dylan went on. "Besides me and Mom, I mean." Brave tipped his head like he knew Dylan was trying to tell him something but he couldn't quite make out the words.

Dylan shooed Brave away from his dad's things and opened the door that led to the kitchen. He held the door open, but Brave hesitated. They blinked at each other for a moment.

"It's okay," Dylan said. "Take your time."

Brave sniffed at the air, stretching his nose toward the inside of the house. Dylan could tell he was curious. Finally, with one last worried look at Dylan, Brave took a step. He paused. Then he took another. Slowly he tiptoed past Dylan into the house and made his way around the perimeter of the kitchen. With his snout hovering a couple of inches off the ground, he explored the tile floor, the baseboards, the crumb-speckled circle under the dinner table. Dylan followed the dog closely. Brave was snuffling along the edge of the refrigerator when a loud crackling noise exploded outside, followed by a series of pops. They both jumped.

It sounded like fireworks—kids in the neighborhood were probably lighting them in a backyard. But before Dylan could reassure Brave, the dog panicked, scuttling across the kitchen floor, his claws scratching on the linoleum. He shot into the living room and—unable to squeeze under the couch—leaped on top of it and desperately scrambled to hide behind the cushions. He burrowed into the back pillows, sending them flying. He kicked and dug his legs under the seat cushions, knocking them to the ground.

"No!" Dylan cried. "Not the couch!" His mom had only bought the sofa a few months ago, and she treated it like it was more than just a piece of furniture. Every night when she came home from work, she lowered herself onto it with a contented smile on her face. Before bed each night she fluffed the cushions, and every couple of days she vacuumed it thoroughly. Even Dylan was barely allowed to sit on the couch, and now there was a dog thrashing around on it.

A dog. In his house.

Dylan's stomach churned as he suddenly realized he'd brought a strange animal into their home. Not just strange, but out of control. Dylan hadn't stopped to consider that maybe Brave had been on his own for so long, he didn't know how to live with people.

"Brave, cut it out!"

But Brave just kept digging deeper into the couch. When a pillow tipped onto his head, he snatched at it with his mouth, clamping his strong jaw tightly around it.

Dylan grabbed the cushion to pull it away from Brave, which only made the dog bite down harder. The harder Dylan pulled, the more Brave pulled back, a wild and terrified look in his eye. Dylan couldn't believe the grip he had on the cushion. Suddenly, with one loud, horrible ripping sound, the whole thing came apart in Dylan's hands. White feathers and yellow clumps of foam flew in every direction, torn to shreds by Brave's sharp teeth.

Dylan's mom had saved up for a year to buy that couch, and now Brave hadn't been there for thirty seconds before he was tearing it apart. What if Dylan couldn't control this dog? There was no way his parents would let him keep it.

Dylan had barely even had time to react when Brave started clobbering another cushion with his paws and jaw. Dylan reached for it, but Brave bit down into it, holding it firmly.

What commands could he give the dog to make him stop?

"Brave—NO!"

Brave's ears shot up in panic, but he didn't release the pillow.

Dylan's brain scrambled for another one. He'd never had a dog before, let alone trained one—he'd only seen trainers giving commands in movies, or read about it in books.

"*Drop it!*" Dylan cried, his voice ringing with desperation.

It was like a miracle. Brave dropped it. His eyebrows scrunched together, and he gazed up at Dylan with a confused look in his eye. He whimpered, a mix of fear and remorse.

"I'm sorry," Dylan said, exhaling in relief. "I didn't mean to shout at you—but the couch . . ." He looked down at the cushion in his hand. What was left of it was a slobbery mess. Feathers and foam floated through the air and settled in a thin coating all around the living room. Dylan's heart pounded in his chest. "Mom's going to freak out!"

Frantically, he started gathering up what was left of the cushion and looking around for a place to hide it. He was heading for the hall closet when he heard Brave scratching and snorting behind him. Dylan spun around with a feeling of dread in the pit of his stomach. The dog was spinning in a circle on the couch, gnawing and pawing at the cushions again.

"No! No, no, no, no, no!" Dylan shouted. "Stop—please just stop!" But Brave ignored him. The dog seemed to be on a quest to destroy the one piece of furniture Dylan's mom really cared about.

Dylan's mind whirled as he tried to figure out how to stop the dog from eating another pillow. Clearly commands were only a temporary solution — what he really needed to do was distract Brave. But was there anything the animal wanted badly enough to make that work?

That was it. There *was* one thing Dylan knew Brave wanted more than anything: food. Brave was starving, right? Dylan raced into the kitchen and grabbed the first thing he saw: a loaf of bread. He ran back into the living room, waving the bag in the air. Could dogs even *eat* bread?

Brave immediately stopped his attack on the couch. Dropping the pillow, he jerked his head up, sniffed the air, and turned to point his snout at Dylan.

"Ah, so you're still hungry, huh?" Dylan said.

Brave snorted to clear his nostrils, but he didn't seem sure about how to get his paws on the food he was smelling. Dylan had to think fast. He crinkled the bag of bread to make some noise. Brave's ears twitched at the sound. Then Dylan removed a slice of bread and chomped off a big bite, exaggerating the sound of chewing.

Now he had the dog's attention.

"This is the best bread I've had in a long time. I bet you'd like it too."

Dylan crinkled the bag again to emphasize the point.

That did the trick. Brave hopped down from the couch and hustled toward him, his nose bobbing on the air tracing the scent of food. As the dog approached, Dylan broke off a piece of bread and held it out. Brave was too skittish to take it from his hand. Dylan placed the chunk of bread on the floor and backed up a few steps, giving Brave some space.

It worked. Brave darted forward, snatched the bread off the ground, and swallowed it in one bite, then retreated a few steps to watch Dylan—and wait for more.

Dylan couldn't believe it—he was actually starting to communicate with Brave. That was the good news. The bad news was that the couch looked like it had been hit by a hurricane—with teeth.

Dylan knew he'd have to clean it up quickly *and* figure out how he was going to explain the mess to his mom. But first he had to get Brave squared away so he couldn't cause any more damage.

Dylan fed Brave some more and led him into his bedroom. The dog circled the room, sniffing the carpet and getting the lay of the land. He seemed calmer now that he'd had something to eat and gotten used to the house a little.

"Don't eat my pillow," Dylan said. "Or my bed. And especially not my baseball glove. Dad gave me that for my birthday."

Just to be sure, Dylan picked up his baseball glove, put it in his sock drawer, and closed it tight.

"Okay, Brave, we have to have some house rules," Dylan said. "I'm technically not allowed to have a dog, but let's just say you're visiting for now. Got it?"

Brave woofed and perked up his soft gray ears, like he was listening to something on a frequency Dylan couldn't hear. A split second later, Dylan heard the front door open.

"Hey, Dyl, I'm home!"

It was his mom.

Dylan's palms went clammy. He hadn't had time to fix the couch or hide the pillows.

Startled by the sound of her voice, Brave was shaking. He jumped up and barked.

"Quiet, Brave!" Dylan whispered. He held a finger to his lips. "It's just Mom. Don't be scared—and keep it down."

Brave watched Dylan's hand and looked confused. Was this some new game? He barked again, louder this time.

Dylan's stomach sank. If Brave kept barking, they were both going to be in huge trouble. Plus, there was already the problem of—

"What happened to my couch!" his mom screeched, her voice rising to a high pitch that reminded Dylan of a fire alarm going off. At the sound of her shouting, Brave hunched down and backed up behind Dylan, until he bumped into the nightstand and couldn't go any further.

Suddenly the bedroom door flew open and Dylan's mom stood there, her face bright red, her arms clutching the remnants of a couch pillow. "Dylan, you'd better have a good reason—"

She froze, her mouth dropping open as her eyes swung from Dylan to the cowering, dirty dog at his feet.

"I can explain," Dylan started to say, but Brave interrupted with a series of barks and growls that took both Dylan and his mom by surprise. Out of nowhere, the dog reared up on his back legs and scratched at the air with his front paws, as if he were fending off an enemy. He landed on all fours and spun around in a tight circle, his whole body vibrating with agitation and excitement. Brave wasn't being aggressive, Dylan realized—he was just scared.

"Dylan!" his mom screamed. Brave froze and dropped into a crouch, his tail down. He looked up at her with a guilty expression on his face.

"Mom—you're scaring him!"

"I'm scaring *him?*" She stopped herself and took a deep, slow breath. When she was calmer, she tried again. This time her voice was low and quiet—the way it got when she was really, really angry. "Dylan. Why. Is. There. A. Dog. In. Your. Bedroom?"

It was worse than Dylan had feared. His mom was pausing after every word. That meant he was in *big* trouble.

"I can explain," he said again. "He's a stray and he was in trouble, and I couldn't just leave him—"

"We can't have an untrained dog in this house," his mom said, her voice getting louder again.

"He's trained," Dylan lied.

His mom held out a piece of torn cushion foam, offering evidence to the contrary.

"Okay, so he's a little rough around the edges," Dylan said.

His mom's voice rose again: "You know what's rough? My couch!" She sounded even angrier. "It's destroyed!"

Out of the corner of his eye, Dylan saw Brave stand up. The dog whimpered and scratched at the floor.

"He's a stray, and he's filthy," his mom finished. Her top lip curled up on the last words.

Just then, the loud popping and crackling sound of fireworks cut through the air again. Dylan's mom squeezed her eyes shut and covered her ears with her hands.

"What is that sound?" she asked through gritted teeth. "What is going *on* around here?"

Before Dylan could reply, Brave's whole body tensed up, and the fur on his back stood on end. For a millisecond, it seemed as if he would just stand there, shaking. But all of a sudden, the dog leaped forward and darted right between Dylan's mom's legs, running out of the bedroom like he knew he was in big trouble. Dylan had wanted to do the same thing many times, but he knew if you ran away from an angry parent, that just made things worse.

"Don't let him loose in my house!" Dylan's mom yelled as they rushed after Brave. But the dog didn't want to stay in the house—he wanted out. Brave ran into the kitchen, searching frantically for the exit. He spotted the sliding door and headed right for it, not knowing that the glass door was open but the screen door was closed.

Brave flung himself at the door, leaping so hard that he knocked the screen right out of its track, and kept going.

Running over the screen on the ground, Dylan dashed out of the house after Brave. He couldn't just let him get away. He'd found a lost dog—or, a dog had found him. That had to be a sign that they were supposed to be together, right?

He just had to make his mom understand that Brave needed him.

"Mom, I'm sorry," Dylan called over his shoulder. "I'll explain later. I just have to catch Brave!"

★ CHAPTER 4 ★

Brave bolted across the yard, around the front of the house, and out into the street, Dylan following close behind, running for all he was worth. But Brave had four legs instead of two, and he was much, much faster.

"Brave, stop!" Dylan shouted.

"Dylan, stop!" his mom shouted, bringing up the rear.

But neither Brave nor Dylan was going to stop. Brave was too spooked by the noise and commotion, and Dylan was too scared to lose Brave. Neither of them was going to listen to anyone or anything.

Brave picked up speed.

This was not going well at all.

At the end of the block, Brave bolted straight across the county road. Dylan held his breath and scanned left and right for traffic. Luckily, there wasn't so much as an approaching car. Brave charged ahead, and Dylan just hoped he would stop when he hit the fence that marked the beginning of the Garcia Ranch. But as the dog approached the barrier, it instantly became clear that nothing was going to stop him. He jumped over the four-foot-high split-rail wood fence like it was nothing at all and raced straight into the Garcias' fields.

Dylan ducked between the rails and through the fence. He felt weird crossing onto their property without permission—it was something he'd always been told not to do. Even though they lived just a few hundred yards away from each other, homeowners and ranchers in San Antonio had different lives, and they didn't always see eye to eye.

Dylan knew he had to respect their property, but he also had to get the dog. He could see Brave running straight across the ranch, past a long barn with a pointed roof and a series of low outbuildings. He was worried the dog would be spotted by a rancher—or, worse, not spotted. Dylan didn't know much about ranch life, but he knew there were dangerous things all over the place. Tractors and heavy machinery. Cattle and horses and who knew what other animals. There were plenty of ways for a dog to get hurt.

As if to confirm Dylan's fear, Brave zigzagged around an idle pickup truck and headed straight for a field teeming with cattle. The dog ducked behind a row of barrels and was out of sight.

"Come back!" Dylan ran at top speed around the truck and followed the sound of Brave's barking. He came around the back of a covered, open-sided building filled with stacks of hay and found himself on the edge of a wide paddock.

At the center of the flat, grassy area, a young girl perched atop the back of a horse. She held on to the reins with one hand and, in the other, swung a rope in the air and flung it outward—toward the leg of a giant-horned bull that clearly did *not* want to be roped. A handful of cowboys leaned on the fence surrounding the corral and cheered her on, whooping and shouting, "Git him!"

Dylan couldn't believe what he was seeing. It looked like a scene from a cowboy movie. The girl on the horse had missed with the rope, so she reeled it back in. She clucked her tongue and tugged on the reins, spinning the horse around in a tight circle. He saw her face screwed up with concentration and realized that he knew her.

It was Grace Garcia. She was in the same grade as him at school, but had a very different friend circle. Grace hung out with what Dylan thought of as the cowboy crew—but what Jaxon called the Ranch Kids. She wore cowboy boots to school every day and let her dark black braid poke out from underneath her cowboy hat and trail down her back.

Grace whistled and called out to a gray and white sheepdog who looked shaggy and sweet but moved with lightning speed and precision. The dog reacted instantly, running in a wide circle around the bull, then closing in closer and closer until it nipped at the bull's back right hoof. It was like Grace was telling her dog what to do, and the dog was passing the message along to the enormous bull. The dog steered the bull into a pen on the far end of the paddock, where a handful of cows stood calmly munching grass. Grace rode up fast and slammed the gate shut behind it. The cowboys erupted in cheers, and Grace broke out in a huge grin.

Dylan had never seen anyone work a bull before, and he was fascinated. How on earth did a girl his age know how to ride a horse and herd cattle—or command a dog like that?

Grace spotted Dylan and blinked, like she was trying to figure out what he was doing there. Before Dylan could say anything, Brave suddenly appeared out of nowhere and shot across the corral, barking like mad and heading straight for the pen—and the bull.

"Brave—no! Stop!" Dylan shouted hopelessly.

But Brave didn't listen. He jumped through the gate, his eyes wide with panic. At the sight of the strange dog, the bull pressed its ears flat back on its head, swished its tail, and stomped its hooves, kicking up dust and making a huge racket. Brave flinched and squatted low to the ground, but he was too scared to move away.

Dylan had always thought of cattle as slow and friendly —at least that's how they were when he saw them in a pasture from a distance. But, he realized then, up close they were huge and strong and kind of scary—and they could hurt him.

"Brave! Get out of there!" Dylan yelled.

"Hyah!" Grace shouted. She dug her heels into her horse's sides and, in one smooth movement, rode to the gate, opened it, and steered her horse into the pen. She positioned herself between the dog and the bull, shielding Brave from the angry animal's hooves. Grace spoke softly to the bull in a calm, soothing voice. The bull raised its head and flicked its tail. Grace was buying Brave time to get out, but Brave didn't understand what was happening. He was just as scared of her and her horse as he was of the bull. In a desperate attempt to get to safety, he darted forward.

But that just put him in more danger.

"Watch it, Brave!" Dylan shouted, but the dog couldn't hear him over the bull's loud snorts and grunts. It was getting more and more agitated, and Dylan watched in horror as it lowered its head and pawed at the ground with its front right hoof. Even Dylan could recognize that as a sign that the animal was getting ready to attack.

The bull flung a back leg out sideways — a warning kick in Brave's direction. Brave yelped and backed up, only to realize he was trapped between Grace's horse, the bull, and a cluster of nearby cows. There was nowhere for him to go. The muscles in the bull's powerful haunches twitched, and it let out one angry snort before raising its back hooves in a half kick off the ground.

"No!" Dylan cried. He couldn't just stand there watching. Without thinking, he dove through the first fence and crossed the paddock in a flash, then ducked through the gate and into the smaller pen. He was under Grace's horse, grabbing Brave by the scruff at the back of his neck and pulling him away from the bull just as the larger animal arched its back and flung its hind legs outward, lifting itself into the air. Slipping and sliding on a patch of muddy ground in the corral, Dylan carried Brave to safety all the way across the ring and outside the fence.

Dylan and Brave flopped down, exhausted and breathing hard. Dylan looked over to find the dog staring at him with big eyes. Still shaking, Brave edged forward and put his head on Dylan's thigh, as if thanking him for his help.

★ CHAPTER 5 ★

Adrenaline still pumped through Dylan's body. He let out a relieved laugh. "You almost got yourself stomped on," he said, giving Brave a good scratch around the ears. Brave licked Dylan's hand over and over as they sat together on the side of the ring.

"That dog needs help," Grace said as she hopped down off her horse and ducked through the fence to join them. She squatted down next to Dylan and reached out to pat Brave.

"I'm so sorry," Dylan said. He felt ridiculous—he and Brave had just appeared out of nowhere and nearly gotten themselves killed on Grace's ranch. "My dog—well, my new dog—well, he's sort of my dog . . ." He stopped and took a breath. "This is Brave, and he's a little out of control. He ran onto your ranch and I followed him. I'm sorry he —we—caused trouble."

Grace raised Brave's chin with her hand and looked him

over. "Seems like your sort of new dog Brave might have a little Blue Lacy in him."

"A lazy?" Dylan asked, unsure of what he had heard.

"Blue Lacy. You know, the Texas state dog."

Dylan didn't know. He'd had no idea states even had dogs—and what were the odds that he'd find one that represented Texas? Wasn't that just further proof that he and Brave were meant to find each other? "That must be why his coat is a little blue."

"Exactly," said Grace. "These dogs are known for their high energy. But it also means they can have a mind of their own."

Dylan had to laugh. Brave definitely had both of those qualities and then some.

Brave looked quickly from one person to the other, his eyes bright and curious.

"He knows we're talking about him," Grace said. Brave blinked at her and stuffed his head into her hand. Dylan could tell that the dog liked her—and that she was good with animals. "How long have you had him?"

"He's actually a stray," Dylan said. "I just found him today."

"Oh, wow. Today? Do you think he has a home?"

Dylan shook his head. "No tags. And he's pretty dirty and hungry."

"Well, let's feed him then." Grace stood, spun around on one booted heel, and headed toward the large ranch house, kicking up dust as she went. Her dog ran along beside her. Dylan wasn't sure at first whether he should follow them until Grace called out "Come on!" without turning back. He scrambled after her, and Brave followed him.

Grace circled around the house to the garage, where a four-door pickup truck and a couple of three-wheel all-terrain vehicles were parked. In a back corner, a fifty-pound bag of dog food leaned against the wall. Grace reached her arm in and pulled out a full scoop of kibble, which she dumped into a nearby bowl.

Brave's eyes practically bugged out of his head at the sight of such a scrumptious meal. He charged forward and nearly inhaled the food. If Dylan hadn't heard crunching, he would have thought the dog wasn't even chewing before he swallowed it.

"Mustang—sit," Grace said to her dog, who looked deeply unhappy not to get to share in the feast. But she obeyed without hesitation. She stayed perfectly still and watched Grace carefully, probably hoping her owner had a treat in mind. "It's not dinnertime for you yet," Grace said.

Brave was done eating almost as soon as he'd started. He slurped water from Mustang's bowl and pawed at the bag of kibble, whining for more.

"Not too much at once," Grace said. "We don't want you to get a stomachache."

Dylan peered out through the open garage door and surveyed the ranch, which sprawled out around them in every direction. "Did you grow up here?"

"Yeah," Grace said. "Three generations of Garcias have lived on this ranch. It was my grandparents' land before it was my parents'."

Dylan thought of his comfortable but small one-story house with its square backyard and tiny front porch. "What's it like? To have all this space, I mean."

"I don't really know any different." She shrugged. "But I love it here — there's a little bit of everything. If you want to be with the horses or the ranch hands you can be. If you want to get away, you can go sit by the creek and be alone. I can't wait to get home after school. It's kind of like its own planet, you know?"

Dylan didn't know, but it sounded pretty great.

"Want a tour?" Grace asked.

"Oh — uh . . . sure. That would be cool."

"Mustang, Brave — come!" The dogs fell in line behind Grace as she led them all out of the garage. Dylan could barely believe his eyes when they circled around the paddock and climbed up a low rise. Below them was a giant field that spread out in every direction. A glimmering creek ran through it, and tall trees lined its perimeter. Beyond the trees were acre upon acre of Texas Hill Country—a tawny tangle of shrubs and trees and rock formations that rose up sharply, then dropped off into shallow valleys and more creek beds. Mustang shot off down the hill and headed for the creek, with Brave right behind her. The dogs splashed into the water and chased each other around.

"It's beautiful," he said.

Grace smiled sadly. "It is. But right now it's also kind of a mess."

At first Dylan wasn't sure what she meant. He shaded his eyes with his hand and squinted down at the field and woods. He scanned the tall grass and tree line. That's when he noticed it. Debris. Everywhere. Splintered tree trunks, piles of plywood, a toppled post-and-rail fence, and even a wrecked outbuilding on the far side of the field. In the woods, the trees that were still standing were bare at the top, stripped of their leaves and smaller branches.

Dylan let out a low whistle. "The hurricane did all this?"

Grace nodded. "But we were lucky. None of us got hurt and all of our animals were safe. Most of our buildings made it too. It's just"—she sighed—"a lot of work to clean up."

"Who's going to do it?"

"Me. My sisters and brother. Everyone." She turned her attention to the creek below, where the dogs were still frolicking. She put her thumb and forefinger into her mouth and let out a whistle so loud that Dylan's ears vibrated. "Mustang! Brave! Come back!" she shouted.

The dogs shot out of the water and up the hill, headed straight for them, sending up a spray of water from their coats as they ran. When the dogs reached Dylan and Grace, they tumbled into a dusty blur at their feet. They were wrestling, and Mustang had her mouth around Brave's snout in a playful hold. Brave had his front paws wrapped around her shoulders and kicked at her with his back legs.

"Ah, Brave!" Dylan cried. "You just gave yourself a bath and now you're getting all dirty again!"

"I guess they like each other." Grace laughed. "He gets along well with other dogs—that's a good sign."

"Is it?" Dylan asked.

Grace shot him a funny look. "Have you ever had a dog before?"

Dylan shook his head, feeling a little sheepish. "Nope." He let out a sad sigh. "And I'm not sure I'm ever going to. I don't think my mom is going to let me keep Brave."

"Why not?"

"Well, he kind of destroyed her couch, and she never agreed to me having a dog, so if we did get one now, he would have to be *really* good. You may have noticed that Brave isn't exactly the best listener."

Even as he said it, Dylan felt his heart twist. He'd only had Brave for a few hours, but already he couldn't imagine giving him up.

"Oh, I don't know," Grace said, studying the Blue Lacy as he hopped up and ran in a wide circle while Mustang chased him. "I think he's a pretty good boy, especially for a stray."

"Really?"

"Yeah. He's not wild or anything. I mean, once he got some food in his belly, he stuck around with us. He followed us out here instead of running off again, and he just came when I called him, didn't he?"

Dylan thought about that for a second. "I guess you're right. But maybe it's not him."

"Huh?"

"Maybe it's you, Grace. He really responds to you. Have you trained a lot of dogs?"

Brave and Mustang ended their chase and, panting heavily, both plopped to the ground and caught their breath. Brave yowled happily and lowered his head onto his paws, as if the day's excitement had caught up to him.

"I trained Mustang," Grace said. "And there are always other dogs around the ranch. Plus I work with horses and cows and all kinds of animals, so I guess I'm pretty comfortable with them."

"That makes sense." Dylan felt Grace's eyes on him, as if she were thinking something over.

"I'll make you a deal," she finally said.

"Okay."

"I'll help you train Brave."

"Wait, what? You will?"

"Sure. It seems like you're already pretty close, so it'd be a bummer if your mom didn't let you keep him."

Dylan wasn't sure what to say, his mind already racing with the possibilities of what it would mean to train Brave and keep him as his own. "That's super nice of you. And that would be awesome. But wait—what's the other part of the deal?"

"I'll help you train Brave if you help me out on the ranch with all the hurricane debris." Grace shrugged like it was a simple exchange.

The offer took Dylan by surprise. He had never worked on a ranch before—the most physical labor he'd ever done was raking leaves on his front lawn. He scanned the debris-strewn field below them, then glanced down at his sneakers. They were fine for school, but now they were caked in mud and—as he'd discovered just a moment before—basically useless for getting around the ranch. He stole a peek at Grace's cowboy boots. They were the real working kind, not the Sunday church kind she usually wore to school.

Dylan suddenly felt self-conscious, his cheeks warm as Grace stared at him. He could definitely use her help with Brave. But how much help could he really be to her?

"Doing cleanup?" he asked uncertainly.

"Don't look so scared." She chuckled at him. "I promise it won't be that hard."

He let out a relieved laugh. "Even for me?"

"Even for you. You could start bright and early tomorrow morning."

"I have to ask my mom. Since I have to convince her first to let me keep Brave."

"Right. Totally."

Dylan considered the offer. It wouldn't be the worst thing to work outside, instead of being stuck inside. It would mean he couldn't hang out with Jaxon, but it wasn't forever—and it was for Brave. If Brave was a good dog, then his mom would have a hard time saying no. "But if my mom says yes, I'll help you, for Brave. Promise."

"For Brave. Pinky swear."

They locked their fingers together to seal the deal, and Brave let out a woof of approval.

★ CHAPTER 6 ★

Dylan and his mom stood in their living room, Brave sitting between them.

Together they looked at the remnants of what had been their couch. Deep scratch marks crisscrossed the seat cushions. The filling of the pillows Brave had destroyed was scattered around the living room like fresh snow.

Dylan looked at his mom. Her face was red with renewed anger, and he knew he was on thin ice. He had to tread carefully if he was going to talk to her about working on the Garcia Ranch and training Brave. Any shot he had depended on how he presented the idea to his mom—and how quickly he could get her to forgive them for the couch incident. Which, at the moment, didn't look too promising.

"Mom, I'm really sorry about th—" Dylan started to stay, but his mom shushed him. She clamped her teeth together and pointed toward the kitchen.

"Broom and dustpan" was all she managed to say.

Dylan didn't argue. He got to work.

While he swept the larger chunks into piles, his mom got the vacuum cleaner and started to work her way through the room, sucking up the smaller pieces and chasing down stray feathers.

When the vacuum cleaner started, Brave startled and rushed to Dylan's side, quaking with fear.

"It's okay, buddy," Dylan said. "It's just the vacuum cleaner. I hate it too." He reached out a hand to comfort the dog, but Brave skittered away.

Dylan's mom turned off the vacuum and wiped sweat from her brow, just as Dylan put the last pieces of cushion into a big garbage bag.

When the vacuum finally stopped, Brave's whole body relaxed. As an experiment, Dylan reached out a hand again. This time, Brave didn't flinch. Dylan lightly brushed the side of the dog's snout with his knuckle, and to his surprise, Brave let him. Dylan forced himself to play it cool so he wouldn't spook the dog, but he was amazed at how soft Brave's fur was. He looked up to see his mom watching them both.

"You said there was a loud noise right before he attacked the couch, right?" she asked.

"Yeah. I think it was fireworks." Dylan had a feeling this line of questioning wasn't going to help his cause—or Brave.

"And he definitely doesn't like the sound of the vacuum cleaner."

"I mean, who does?" Dylan knew it sounded silly the second the words exited his mouth.

His mom's face softened. "Honey, I get that you really like this dog, but he's awfully skittish."

Dylan saw an opening. "Right now he is, but you should have seen him on the ranch today—he was great! He really got along well with Grace Garcia's dog, Mustang, and Grace really knows dogs and she said—"

"Dylan—"

"—he's a good dog but just needs some training and—"

"*Dylan*—"

"It's just because he's a stray, that's all. He needs to get used to the new sounds and people. He just needs a minute—"

"Dylan!" his mom said loudly. "Stop. That's all great, but we don't know for sure that he's even a stray."

"Wait—no." Dylan shook his head emphatically. "No way. He was living behind the taco place—"

"Still." His mom held up both hands to stop him. "What if he has a family who's looking for him right this second?

Wouldn't it be best for him if we try to find out whether he has a home? Doesn't he deserve to be with the people he loves and trusts?"

Dylan looked down at Brave, who sat quietly as if he were listening to their conversation. His soft amber eyes locked on Dylan's. Dylan held out a hand to the dog, who sniffed his knuckles—then gave them one quick lick.

What if someone was looking for him?

"So as soon as we're done here," his mom continued, "we'll take him over to the shelter and see if anyone has been looking for him."

"Wait—the shelter?" Dylan gasped. "What? Why— Can't we just keep him here and put up flyers or something?"

"No," she said firmly. "Because whether or not he has a family, Dyl, I think it's very possible Brave has had some kind of trauma. And that means we don't really know him, or what kind of dog he is."

Dylan flashed back to his first sight of Brave, cowering behind the dumpster. The dog had been terrified, it was true. But he was also quick to follow Dylan home, which meant he was trusting, and he responded to Grace, which meant he was trainable. "Mom—" he started to argue, but she cut him off.

"We're taking him to the shelter, Dylan." She took a

breath to calm herself. "Please don't argue with me. It's the right thing to do."

Dylan's heart sank. "Is this because he's not trained?" he asked, grasping at anything. "Because Grace said she'd help me train him—"

"I mean . . ." His mom gestured at the remains of their couch. "I'm not going to lie. That's a big part of it."

"I'll train him—you'll see!"

"Dylan, enough! You know we can't keep that dog."

"He's not *that dog*, Mom. His name is Brave."

"Okay, fine, we can't keep *Brave*. He's already destroyed part of the house, and he could have another name and another family who's looking for him, you know?"

Dylan wanted to protest, but what could he really say?

If he had a dog like Brave and they had gotten separated, he'd be heartbroken—and he'd want him to come home too.

★ CHAPTER 7 ★

"Nope. No chip." The woman at the animal shelter dropped the rectangular plastic scanner into her pocket. "But that doesn't mean he doesn't belong to someone. It could just mean that they never microchipped him. A lot of pet owners don't." She let out an annoyed snort. "I wish everyone would."

"So does that mean we should take him home?" Dylan asked hopefully.

"Not exactly," the woman said. "We can keep him here and see if anyone comes looking for him. But . . ." she hesitated. "We're overloaded with hurricane dogs."

"Hurricane dogs?" Dylan wasn't exactly sure what she meant.

"Dogs that got separated or lost during the storm," the woman said matter-of-factly. "It's always a problem after a whopper like the one we had, but this time was especially bad. So we can only keep him for two weeks."

"And then what?" Dylan asked.

The woman and his mom exchanged a look.

"Let's just wait and see," Dylan's mom said, putting an arm around his shoulders. "Someone could come looking for him by then."

"Come on, pal." The woman reached out to pick up Brave, but he pulled away from her and pressed himself against Dylan's body. Without thinking, Dylan wrapped his arms around the dog, who shook with fear but didn't fend him off.

"Dylan, sweetie . . ." his mom said. "They'll take good care of him here."

"I got him," the woman said, slipping her arms between Dylan and the dog. Dylan had no choice but to release his hold on Brave and let the woman pick him up.

Dylan reached out and stroked the top of Brave's head, aware—and sad—that Brave was really starting to trust him just as they were saying goodbye.

"Bye, buddy."

Brave looked up at him with an expression of such confusion and fear that it nearly broke Dylan's heart. The woman turned and headed through a swinging door. She pushed it open with her shoulder and paused, turning back to speak to Dylan and his mom.

"Make sure you leave your number at the front desk, and we'll call you if anyone comes to claim him."

But Dylan barely heard what she was saying. He was too busy staring past her, into a room lined floor to ceiling with kennels. Each one had a metal gate latched tightly shut —and each one contained a dog that looked just as lonely and scared as Brave.

The place was packed. There had to be dozens of dogs there, in cages just big enough for them to turn around in. It was the saddest thing Dylan had seen in his whole life.

As soon as the swinging door opened, the dogs broke out in a series of barks so loud and insistent that it was nearly overpowering. Dylan's hands flew to his ears, but not before he heard the single most desperate howl of all: the one coming from Brave's throat. The dog was petrified, shaking and frantically scrambling to get out of the shelter worker's arms.

Horrified, Dylan turned to his mom. Her face was pale, and her jaw hung open.

Mom, we can't leave him here, he mouthed to her.

She nodded. "I know."

★ ★ ★

His mom steered the car out of the parking lot and glanced at him in the rearview mirror.

"Two weeks—that's it, Dyl," she said.

Dylan sat in the back seat with Brave. "Okay! Thank you!"

"That means we can foster him for two weeks *max*, but you're going to need to take care of him."

"I know, Mom. Thank you."

"That means you're going to have pay for his food and any trips to the vet, too."

"I know, Mom." Dylan was so happy that Brave was coming home with them that he would have agreed to anything in that moment.

"And you need to get him trained. Like, right away, because I will not be losing another piece of furniture."

"I will. I told you — Grace is going to help me."

"Grace? You mentioned her earlier — you guys have been in school together for a long time, right?"

"Right. She's Mr. Garcia's daughter. She's really great with animals."

His mom raised an eyebrow but kept her eyes on the road. "And she's just going to help you train him? That's nice of her."

"Well . . ." Dylan trailed off. He hadn't had a chance to tell his mom yet about the deal he'd made with Grace. "I kind of agreed to give her a hand in exchange. On the ranch."

They had stopped at a red light, and his mom twisted around fully in her seat to look at him. "You're going to work on a ranch?" She grinned at him. "You won't even pick up the clothes on your floor."

His mom's words stung, even though Dylan knew it was true. He wasn't always great at staying on top of his chores and helping out around the house, and he and his mom argued about it—a lot. But this time, things were different. This time, he had a dog to save.

This wasn't for Dylan—it was for Brave.

Plus, there was the second part of his plan, which Dylan was keeping to himself for the time being. If he could train Brave as much as possible in the next two weeks, his mom would see what a great dog he was and fall in love with him. Then they could keep him forever. If no one went to the shelter looking for him, that was.

"I'm going to get him totally trained. Cross my heart! And cross Brave's heart, too."

Dylan looked down at Brave, who was exhausted from his long, exciting day. He gave a quick wag of his tail and yawned, letting out a sleepy yowl. His eyes were bright, though, as if he were listening to every word they said. Brave didn't understand what was going on, but he could sense that Dylan was excited about something, and that made him excited too.

"You're sure you know what you're getting into?" Dylan's mom asked.

"How hard could it be?" Dylan said.

"Famous last words, kiddo." His mom shook her head. "But we have a deal. When does Grace want you to start?"

"Tomorrow morning."

"Well, don't forget to set your alarm. Ranch life starts bright and early, you know."

Dylan groaned. "Yeah, I know. Grace mentioned that already," he said. "But you know me: early to bed, early to *something*."

Dylan couldn't remember the rest of the expression, but it didn't matter. They had pulled into their driveway, and he was already leading Brave inside, excited to share the good news with his dad.

★ CHAPTER 8 ★

Dylan sat on his bed and patted the spot next to him for Brave to lie down.

Brave circled the bed, sniffing and unsure.

"It's okay, boy," Dylan reassured him.

They stared at each other for a second. Finally, Brave hopped up and stood next to Dylan on the bed, scoping out the view from a new height. Dylan had done his best to give the dog a real bath, and he smelled clean for once — though Dylan had to admit that there was more water on the bathroom floor than on the dog. But he'd cleaned it all up and had even put all the wet towels straight into the washing machine. A promise was a promise, and he wanted to give his mom every reason to trust that he would live up to his end of their bargain.

Brave nosed at Dylan's pillow and scratched at the covers, bunching them up under his paws. He spun around a few times, then spun back in the other direction. Finally, he lay down at Dylan's side. Dylan wanted to throw his arms around the dog and pull him in for a hug, but he resisted the urge. Instead, he tapped the little video camera icon next to his dad's number. They tried to talk as much as possible, but it was sometimes tough to catch each other with school and mission schedules and time differences. They sent video messages back and forth a few times a week, but when something special came up, it was way better to have a live chat.

And what could be more special than meeting Brave?

Dylan framed himself and Brave in the camera while the line rang.

There was a beep, a click, some scratchy noises, and then suddenly his dad's face appeared on the screen. That first sight of his dad, in motion and full color, always made Dylan's heart skip a beat. It was almost as good as seeing him in person. Almost.

"Dyl! What the—"

"Hi, Dad! I wanted you to meet someone."

His dad's eyes bugged out. "Dude! There's a dog in your bed! In my house! What is happening back there?"

Dylan laughed. "It's chaos without you."

"I can see that. Seriously—who is this fine feathered creature?"

"He's furry, for one. And his name is Brave."

"Brave. Huh." His dad leaned forward and squinted into the camera. "Give me a better look at him, would you?"

Dylan waved the phone around so his dad could see Brave from every angle. Brave half raised one paw, cocked an eyebrow, and checked out the phone suspiciously, like he couldn't trust it.

Dylan's dad whistled. "That's one fine-looking dog, Dyl. Is he . . . kind of bluish? Or do we have a bad connection?"

"Nope, he's blue all right. Blue-gray. He's called a Blue Lacy."

"Oh yeah," his dad said, sitting back in his chair. "The state dog of Texas. Hunters, right?"

"So you knew about them too?"

"Sure. But Dylan?"

"Yeah?"

His dad dropped his voice to a whisper. "Does your mom know there's a dog in your room?"

"Ha, funny, Dad."

"Seriously, though—I know how your mother feels about dogs. And it's not great. So where exactly did this guy come from and how did you convince her to let him into the house? Tell me everything—go."

Dylan took a deep breath and, in one long stream of words, told his dad the whole story—from meeting Brave at the restaurant, to the torn-up couch, to Grace and the bull, to the depressing scene at the shelter, to his plan to train Brave while they fostered him. He left out the part about hoping his mom would get so attached to Brave that they could keep him. One step at a time.

"I'm proud of you, Dyl," his dad said.

"You are?"

"Sure. Not about the couch part—that's not good at all, and we're going to have to figure out a way for you to pay your mom back."

Dylan knew he was getting off easy on that count.

"But you're really stepping up to take care of Brave, and that's a big commitment. I can tell how much you want to make it work. That takes effort."

There was a funny feeling in Dylan's chest, and he couldn't help but smile. "Thanks, Dad."

Being separated from his dad was the hardest thing in Dylan's life, no question. But every once in a while, when they managed to steal a minute to see each other onscreen and talk in real time, it felt like they were together.

"By the way, I think he likes you." His dad pointed at Brave.

Dylan looked down at his side. He hadn't noticed, but Brave had fallen asleep next to him, with his head leaning against Dylan's leg. He was snoring loudly.

"Dogs snore?" Dylan stage-whispered to his dad, stifling a laugh.

"Sure dogs snore." His dad guffawed. "They're exhausted just like the rest of us."

Dylan stifled a yawn just as his dad spoke.

"Speaking of which," his dad said. "Time for you to hit the hay, bud. I love you."

"I love you too, Dad. Talk to you later."

They clicked off the call, and Dylan lay there for a second, enjoying the feeling of Brave's chest rising and falling. He started to replay the day, reliving everything that had happened since he and Jaxon had bought water balloons. But before he knew it, he was snoring too, the phone facedown on his chest, one arm resting lightly on the dog asleep next to him.

★ CHAPTER 9 ★

Dylan's arm was numb. He woke up to find it stretched out at an odd angle, with Brave snoozing soundly in the crook of his elbow. He eased himself out from under Brave's head and shook out his arm, which quickly became all pins and needles. Brave's ears twitched, but he otherwise didn't move.

The dream Dylan had just been having came back to him. He was a cowboy in the Old West, and Brave was his dog. Dylan had been riding a horse and lassoing cattle while Brave ran out ahead of him, nipping at a cow's ankles. It was an awesome dream, and Dylan wished he could start it up again to see what happened next. He rolled over on his side. Brave was warm, and Dylan realized how relaxing it was to have a dog sleeping next to him. So relaxing that he thought maybe he should just go back to bed for a few minutes. His eyelids slid closed.

Dylan dozed for ten more minutes, until he was

awakened by a muffled *ding!* from his phone, which had migrated underneath him during the night. He fumbled for it, opened one eye, and saw a text from his dad:

Good luck on your first day of training! Love you.

Training? Dylan thought, his mind still groggy.

His eyes shot open. Training!

Dog training!

He'd totally forgotten.

Dylan jumped up, and Brave tumbled out of bed after him. The dog went from asleep to alert and ready in an instant. As Dylan dashed around the room throwing on clothes, Brave followed fast on his heels, his tail up and wagging and his ears flicking at every new sound — a drawer opening, a closet door slamming. Dylan wasn't used to having a dog, and he could already see that the dog reacted to his energy. The more excited he was, the more excited the dog became.

They raced down to the kitchen. Dylan's mom was already at work — she ran a research lab and had some experiments that often needed attention on the weekends. Dylan grabbed two breakfast bars — one for him and one for the dog.

"Come on, Brave!" He ran to the sliding glass door and flung it open, expecting Brave to run through it. When he didn't, Dylan turned to look back.

Brave was in the middle of the kitchen, his ears up, his front paws splayed out and his chest lowered to the floor. His rump was up in the air and his tail wagged like it was supercharged. He jumped up to all fours, spun around in a circle, then lowered himself back down again.

"You think we're playing a game!" Dylan laughed. "We don't have time for this, buddy. Come on—let's go." Brave whimpered in response, and his expression changed from playful to serious as he scratched at the floor with one front paw. Dylan studied him for a second, trying to interpret the message. He looked down at the breakfast bar in his hand, and it clicked. "You're starving!" Dylan said. "Sorry, Brave, but we're going to eat breakfast on the road today. Come on!"

He took a step toward the door, but Brave didn't budge. Dylan was starting to get stressed—they were getting later by the second. Then he remembered what had happened with the bread the day before. Dylan fumbled with the wrapper on the bar and ripped open the packaging. He broke off a piece, showed it to Brave, then dropped it on the floor at his feet. That did the trick. The dog raced forward, chomped down the breakfast bar, and stared up at Dylan, anxiously waiting for more. Dylan stepped backward through the sliding glass door into the yard, and Brave followed, whining. Dylan put a second piece down on the ground, and the dog came forward to eat it.

A bird squawked loudly in the tree that towered over their yard, and Brave's head shot up toward the sound. His ears flicked, his nose twitched, and his whole body tensed up.

"Over here," Dylan said, trying to get the dog's attention again. He crinkled the foil wrapper, and Brave turned back to him.

Dylan hopped on his bike and pedaled it so slowly, he had to zigzag to stay upright. They made their way out of the yard and down the street like this, with Dylan luring Brave on, bite by bite, until the bar was down to crumbs. Every couple of minutes, Brave would get distracted again —by another bird, a cat in a neighbor's window, a truck downshifting as it rounded the corner. Even with the food as a bribe, Brave was hard to keep on track. Dylan knew it was going to be a lot of work to train the dog, and he prayed their day on the ranch would go smoothly—aside from the fact that they were already super late.

"When did you get a dog, dude?"

Dylan dropped his feet to the ground to stop his bike and spun around at the familiar voice. Jaxon was sitting on his bike in the middle of the street, his arms crossed over his chest and an amused look on his face as he stared down at Brave.

"Oh, hey, Jax," Dylan said. "Yeah I sort of got a dog. Yesterday after I left the ninety-nine-cent store. It's a long story." A long story that Dylan didn't have time to explain right then. "This is Brave. He's really cool—"

"I didn't know you were into dogs," Jaxon said with a shrug. "You ready?"

Dylan was confused for a second. "Ready for wha—" he started to say, and then he remembered. Water balloons. They were supposed to throw water balloons at cars. He had told Jaxon he'd be there, but that was before Brave. "Oh, man, I'm sorry, Jaxon, but I can't do it today."

"What?" Jaxon asked as if he'd heard Dylan wrong. "No way."

"I have to train Brave."

"You have to train Brave?" Jaxon said incredulously. "You mean the dog you 'sort of got' yesterday afternoon—after you *promised* me you'd do this with me?" He paused for effect. "Not cool."

Dylan swallowed hard. Jaxon was right—he'd said he would be there, and it wasn't okay for him to go back on his word, was it? But he had also promised Grace he would be at the ranch first thing in the morning, and he was already late. He really needed her help with Brave.

Dylan froze, not sure what to do. He looked down at

Brave, who stared back at him with bright eyes and his mouth hanging open, waiting for another piece of food or some kind of sign that they were going to get moving again.

"Dude," Jaxon pressed him. "What're you waiting for? It's going to be so cool! You can go train the dog after."

Dylan's head was spinning, and he felt like he was physically being pulled in two directions at once. He didn't want to throw water balloons at cars—that much he knew. But this was his best friend, and the last thing he wanted was for Jaxon to start giving him a hard time or, worse, telling their friends that Dylan was boring. Plus, he told himself, maybe Jax was right. Maybe he could do both things. He was already late to the ranch after all, so what was the big deal if he was just a little bit later? That way he could go with Jaxon *and* train Brave with Grace.

"You're right. Let's go."

"Good call, Dyl." With a loud whoop, Jaxon pumped a fist in the air and took off down the street.

Dylan followed behind, Brave running alongside him.

They rode to the other side of the neighborhood, and Jaxon stopped his bike on the walkway of a two-lane bridge. Dylan pulled over next to him and leaned over the railing. A wave of dizziness washed over him as he looked straight down at the cars, zipping along the underpass below. He checked the time on his phone—he really needed to hurry this along.

"You have the balloons?" Dylan asked.

"Filled and ready." Jaxon pulled a sealed plastic baggie from his backpack. It was stuffed with taut water balloons so full they looked like they were about to pop. "This is going to be amazing—we are *totally* going viral! Don't throw any until I get my camera ready, okay?"

"Okay." Dylan exhaled slowly.

Jaxon opened the bag and held it out. Reluctantly, Dylan took one of the balloons, while Jaxon grabbed two with one hand and grinned like a cat who had a solid lead on a mouse. He put the bag down and got out his phone. Brave watched them both curiously, then, following the sound of traffic below, stuck his head through the railing and looked down.

"On three?" Jaxon's eyes sparkled with anticipation.

Dylan wished he could be as excited about what they were about to do as his friend was, but instead he just felt pressured. Dylan hefted the balloon in his left hand, preparing to toss it over the side of the bridge and forcing himself to look like he was having fun. But he wasn't.

It was a feeling he'd never had before. He and Jaxon had been friends for so long that they were as used to each other as brothers—and Dylan couldn't remember a single time when they didn't have a blast together. This feeling wasn't normal, just as what they were about to do wasn't normal.

But there he was.

"One." Jaxon began counting. "Two." He pulled his arm back, ready to launch the projectile. Dylan did the same. "*Three!*"

Jaxon launched a balloon, but Dylan didn't. Jaxon held his phone in his other hand and filmed the missile as it arced out over the cars below, then nailed the roof of an SUV with a loud splat. The car slowed for a second, and Dylan saw the driver lean forward and peer up through the windshield at them, just before she passed underneath the bridge. He hated the startled—and not happy—look on her face, but he was relieved that she hadn't swerved or slammed on the brakes.

"That was awesome!" Jaxon cried. "What are you waiting for, Dyl? Go! Do it!"

Dylan swallowed the lump in his throat. He looked down at Brave, who still stood with his head through the railing, watching the cars below. The dog's body was tensed up, and his tail hung down.

Here goes nothing, Dylan thought. He watched a minivan approach and did some mental math to time his toss carefully. He wanted to hit the van as close to its back end as possible, or, if he got it just right, maybe he could even manage to miss it entirely. He'd never tried to bungle a shot before—but he'd also never thrown a missile at a moving vehicle before. His arm shaking, Dylan silently counted down.

He launched the water balloon through the air. It sailed downward in a graceful motion and hit the pavement just behind the minivan, leaving a water stain on the asphalt. *Perfect,* Dylan thought.

"Ah, so close!" Jaxon said. He turned the camera on Dylan's face. "What do you have to say about your aim, young man?" he asked, like a news announcer.

Dylan swatted the camera away. "Not my best throw," he said, trying to smile and play along.

Jaxon took a few turns and got a few angry shouts from drivers. Then it was Dylan's turn again.

"Show us what you got—go again!" Jaxon commanded him, stepping back so he could get a wide shot. The camera made Dylan feel even worse—he hated that this was being recorded, and the thought of someone watching the video made him feel sick to his stomach. He took another balloon from the bag and looked over the side of the bridge. Brave looked up at him, his brow furrowed as if to ask what Dylan was about to do.

Dylan watched a pickup truck. Jaxon swung the camera around and captured the truck's approach. "There's our target," Jaxon narrated. He turned the lens back on Dylan. "And there's our hero, preparing to make the perfect shot . . ."

Dylan eyed the truck and tried to tune out Jaxon's voice. His arm was cocked and ready, but he waited a second. Then another.

"Dude!" Jaxon said. "You're going to miss it! What are you waiting for?"

Dylan launched the water balloon a split second before he wanted to, and it burst open on the driver's-side window with a loud popping sound.

Then it all happened at once. The pickup truck screeched to a sudden stop, its nose pulling hard to the right. Brave flinched at the sound and backed away from the railing, barking like mad, then shot off the bridge and down the street. And Dylan saw the driver of the truck rolling down the window so he could find the source of the object that had just hit his car.

"Run!" Jaxon screamed. "Go go go go go!"

Dylan was on his bike in a flash, racing off after Brave. The boys tried to put as much distance between themselves and the truck as possible. Dylan's heart was pounding hard with fear, and he half expected to see the truck come racing around the corner ahead of them at any second, blocking their path. But no one appeared.

They seemed to have gotten away with it.

He caught up to Brave.

"It's okay, boy," Dylan called out to the dog. Brave's ears flicked toward the sound of his voice, and Dylan rode alongside him. "Come on, Brave. This way." Dylan turned the corner and was relieved to see that Brave followed him.

Jaxon hooted loudly as he pedaled hard, pulling ahead of them. Dylan stared at his friend's back, wondering who this person was now—and how he could seem so happy about what they had just done.

★ CHAPTER 10 ★

By the time Dylan got to the ranch it was almost lunch-time. Panting and sweating, Dylan just wanted to get to work with Brave and forget everything else about that morning.

They pulled through the wrought-iron archway with GARCIA RANCH written across the top, and Brave trot-ted along. He seemed happy to be back in a familiar place. Dylan pedaled down the dirt road that wove through the property and headed for the corral, looking for Grace.

As they passed the barn, Dylan peered inside and saw a small forklift carrying a pallet stacked high with wooden fenceposts. The engine whirred as the driver lowered the heavy load, setting it down with a thundering, ear-busting boom.

Brave lost it. He let out a terrified yelp and crouched down low on all fours, his tail down and his ears back. He howled once more, then suddenly shot off around the side of the building and out of sight.

"Brave—no!" Dylan shouted. "Ugh—not again!" He knew that they'd gotten lucky the day before, and that probably wasn't going to happen twice. If he couldn't stop Brave, then the dog could get trampled for real this time.

Dylan pedaled after him, but Brave was too fast. As Dylan rounded a corner, Brave far in the lead, Grace suddenly appeared up ahead, blocking the dog's path. She crouched down and reached out to Brave just as he ran by, wrapping her arms around his chest and stopping him in his tracks. Brave shook in her arms but didn't try to get away.

"Grace! Hey! Sorry about that, um, again . . ." Dylan said, riding up to Grace and hopping off his bike. "There was a really loud sound in the barn and he panicked."

"That'll get a dog in trouble on a ranch," said Grace with a shake of her head. She didn't make eye contact with Dylan. "Why are you here, though?"

"I'm late! I'm sorry," Dylan felt his face go red. "I was just hanging with Jaxon. Do you know him?"

"Sure," Grace said. "Everyone knows Jaxon. You really hang out with him? Why?"

Dylan was surprised by the question. "We've been friends since we were little," he said. "He's fun." He noticed the defensiveness in his own voice.

"Fun. Right. Whatever you say," Grace said evenly. She released Brave, who had calmed down and was sitting quietly. Grace stood up. "So what can I do for you?"

Dylan was confused. Had she forgotten? "I came to get Brave trained," Dylan said shyly. "I mean, if the offer's still on the table."

"It was on the table," Grace said. "But the table was cleared about two hours ago."

She checked the time on her phone, and Dylan's cheeks went even hotter.

"If you want my help then you have to follow through and be on time. If you can't even follow directions, how is Brave supposed to?"

Dylan was used to getting in trouble when he ignored his chores or forgot his homework, and it wasn't a feeling he liked. But this wasn't a messy room or a missed assignment. Now things were serious. If Grace didn't help him, then Brave would have to go back to the shelter. He could have kicked himself for making the decision to go with Jaxon and throw water balloons. What had he been thinking? Right now, getting Brave trained was more important than anything else.

He searched for the right words, finally settling on the simplest. "I'm really sorry, Grace. I promise I'll never be late again. I really want to train Brave—I need to train him. Can you please help me?"

Brave barked like he knew his fate depended on winning Grace over. She looked down at him and held out a hand for him to sniff. He licked her palm.

"All right, fine." Grace sighed. "But two strikes, you're out around here—that's the Garcia family way."

"Got it. Two strikes." Dylan gulped.

"And we have to get you suited up first." She nodded toward his shorts and sneakers. "You can't move tree branches in that."

Dylan and Brave followed Grace toward the main house.

"You guys dress like cowboys all the time?" he asked. "Seems like a lot of stuff to put on every day."

"Everything we wear has a purpose," Grace said. "For work. You'll see once we get out there."

They climbed the steps to the back porch of the house, where a pile of gear waited for them.

"These are called chaps," Grace said, holding up what looked like a pair of leather pants—if pants only covered the fronts of your legs. "They keep your legs safe around the cattle and the muck."

"What's the muck?" Dylan asked.

Grace grinned. "You'll see."

She gave Dylan instructions for how to get into each piece of gear, bracing him as he pulled on a pair of her brother's old cowboy boots, showing him how to tie the belt on the leather chaps, and finally giving him a real cowboy hat to keep the sun out of his eyes. Brave scuttled around him in circles, yipping at him, wanting to get in on the action.

Once he was fully suited up, Grace stepped back to admire him and gave him a double thumbs-up. But Dylan just felt awkward and clumsy. He took a step toward Grace, and the heavy chaps dropped to the ground around his feet. The belt was too big for him.

Dylan scrambled to pull up the chaps and cinched the belt as tight as it would go. The cowboy boots hurt. Their soles were rock hard and flat compared to the sneakers he usually wore. And the cowboy hat kept tipping forward into his eyes and blinding him.

Grace looked him over, inspecting the gear. "They're a little big on you, but it's good enough to get you started."

Good enough? No way. Dylan felt small and lost in the giant, unfamiliar clothes. He frowned, wishing there was a better way to get Grace's help, one that didn't include him feeling ridiculous.

"Don't worry," Grace said. "You'll get the hang of everything."

Dylan took a breath and hiked up his belt. A promise was a promise, and he couldn't quit on Brave. "Including the chaps?" he asked.

"Including the chaps." Grace grinned. "Now we have to get some duds for Brave." She pulled a piece of rope from her back pocket and tied an adjustable knot into it, then slipped it over Brave's head. It was a makeshift collar. Dylan realized he should have thought to buy one for Brave—and a leash, too. That was like Dog 101, wasn't it?

Grace held out a small, dog-size leather vest and a bright red bandanna. "He needs protecting too."

"How does a bandanna protect a dog?" Dylan asked.

"It's bright colored, so it makes him easier to see around here."

As Brave squirmed and wiggled, Dylan helped angle his front legs through the armholes in the vest and knotted the bandanna around his neck. The dog seemed about as comfortable with the whole outfit as Dylan was with his. Cowboy gear looked impressive when you saw it in a movie, Dylan thought, but when it was actually on your body, it was a whole different deal. He tried to focus on the goal: Even looking this silly would be worth it when Brave was perfectly trained and could live with him forever.

He looked down to see Brave nipping at his new vest,

shaking his head back and forth violently, and swiping at the scarf with his front leg, trying desperately to get it off his neck.

"Brave! Take it easy, boy," Dylan called, but Brave wasn't listening.

"You need to show him how to behave," Grace said.

For a second, Dylan wasn't sure what she was saying. How was he supposed to show a dog how to act? Get down on all fours and bark? Then he remembered what Grace had said when they showed up late. *If you can't even follow directions, how is Brave supposed to?*

Dylan understood. He needed to show Brave that even if you weren't comfortable, you just had to get on with it.

Brave was yapping and jumping around on his front paws. Dylan tugged on his belt and readjusted his hat.

"I guess it's time to get to work," he told Grace.

"You bet, cowboy," Grace said.

Grace hopped off the porch and headed toward the fields, with Dylan trailing right behind. He looked back over his shoulder at Brave, and sure enough, the moment the dog realized Dylan was leaving, he stopped spinning in circles and rushed to follow along.

★ CHAPTER 11 ★

"Seriously, Brave?" Dylan dropped an armful of tree branches onto the pile, wiped the sweat from his brow, and looked down at the dog. Brave had a stick in his mouth and was pawing at Dylan's leg, ready for a game of tug-of-war. Dylan waved a hand at the field strewn with debris. "You see all this? I've got work to do. No time for playing, pal."

They had only cleared a corner of the huge field and had a long way to go before they could even stop for a snack.

Brave whined, dropped to the ground a few feet away, and busied himself with gnawing on one end of the stick. Grace's dog, Mustang, sidled over and plopped down next to Brave. She took the other end of the stick in her mouth and the two dogs chewed side by side. Dylan had to admit that it was pretty sweet that the dogs already got along so well.

Grace walked up and tossed a load of branches onto the stack.

"You're not tired already, are you?" she said to Dylan.

He exhaled and put his hands on his hips. "How are you *not* tired?" Dylan asked. "This is harder than I thought it would be—and remember, you promised it wouldn't be too hard."

"I'm a rancher's daughter," Grace said with a shrug. "You'll get used to it. If you plan to stick around past day one, that is."

Dylan rolled his eyes at her. "I plan to stick around."

"Just checking," Grace said. "You look like you'd rather be home playing video games, that's all."

"Well, I'd definitely rather be doing that," Dylan cracked. "But I'm not going anywhere."

Brave barked and Dylan felt something tugging on his leg. He twisted around to look behind him. The dog was jumping forward and back, nipping at Dylan's chaps and trying to pull him away to play.

"Brave!" Dylan swatted at the dog, but Brave skittered away and lowered his chest to the ground, his tail wagging high in the air. "Not now. Later, pal." Dylan shook his head.

"He's got a lot of energy," Grace observed. She was squinting at Brave, sizing him up. "Mustang was like that too when she was a pup." Mustang rolled onto her back on the grass, her paws in the air. She closed her eyes and basked in the midday sun. "Maybe Brave is still young."

"The people at the shelter thought he was almost two. Is that young?"

She nodded. "For a dog it is. Some still act like puppies until they're three."

As if on cue, Brave swung his head in a circle, tossing the stick up in the air and chasing after it. Dylan and Grace both laughed and got back to work.

"Help me with this one, would you?" Grace waved Dylan over to a long, thick tree trunk lying on the ground. It was too heavy for her to pick up on her own. He grabbed one end and she grabbed the other.

"Three . . . two . . ." Grace counted down. "One!" They lifted at the same time and raised the heavy wood off the ground. They stumbled quickly toward the pile and, with a swing, heaved it onto the tall stack of tangled dry branches. Twigs and leaves went flying as the tree trunk crashed onto the pile. It snapped through the layers with a loud *pop! pop! pop!* before hitting the bottom with a dull thud.

Brave let out a terrified yelp. Dylan spun toward him and saw that the dog was trembling with fear, a line of fur standing on end on his back. He had dropped the stick and there was a wild look in his eye.

"What's up, buddy?" Dylan asked. He took a step toward

the dog, but Brave backed away. Dylan squatted down and reached out a hand, trying to lure the dog over to him. But Brave was beyond reach.

"He's terrified," Grace said under her breath to Dylan. "He's about to bolt, but we can catch him. I'll go left, you go right. But go slow."

Dylan nodded. He stepped slowly to the right while Grace moved in the opposite direction. They flanked Brave, who stared at the ground, panting in short, sharp breaths. They got within arm's reach, but that seemed too close for comfort for the dog, who took one desperate look around, then tried to run past them. Grace managed to snatch his collar just as he flew past. At first Brave strained against her grip, but soon he gave up, whimpering and shuffling his front paws in an anxious dance. Dylan ran over and dropped to his knees by Grace's side. He reached out for Brave, who let Dylan stroke his head and back while he trembled.

"Shhhhh," Dylan whispered. "Shhhhh. It's okay, Brave."

Grace was silent for a long moment, thinking. She assessed Brave from snout to paws. "It's like he had some kind of really bad experience and it's made him extra jumpy."

"The shelter said they got a ton of dogs after the hurricane," Dylan said. "Dogs that got lost or separated from their families."

"That's so sad," Grace said.

"I know. The place was packed—there were so many dogs there, it was awful." Dylan ran a hand down Brave's back and scratched him on the side. "Do you think Brave could be one of them?"

"That could explain it," Grace said with a nod.

"Or if he was a stray, then he might have been out in the storm." Dylan shuddered. Every time he thought of the hurricane, he felt the same fear he'd felt that night and relived the awful noise of it. He remembered how it felt when the house shook, or how he jumped every time a tree branch or potted plant slammed into the side of his house. He remembered the endless sound of the rain beating down on the roof and sideways into the windows. Sometimes Dylan's adrenaline started pumping at the mere memory of it all, and he had to remind himself that it was over and he was safe.

He couldn't imagine what it would have been like to be outside during that storm. Alone. Without any understanding of what was happening. Just like Brave and any of the other animals who were lost or stranded by the hurricane.

It was a horrible, chilling thought. Were those the images running through Brave's mind every time he heard a loud noise? Was he feeling the rain against his fur or hearing the wind beating in his ears again? Dylan hated the thought of Brave going through something that awful—something so bad that it still upset him. But he also knew that if the dog didn't get over it, there was no way he'd be able to stay with Dylan and his family.

"So . . . what do we do?" he asked.

"The first thing we need to do is train him," Grace said. "That'll help you bond with him. And then he'll trust you and listen to you more, even if he's upset."

"That sounds like a good plan," Dylan said.

"Let's start with the basics," Grace said. "Sit, stay, and come."

"Yeah, um, he's not great with commands," Dylan said sheepishly. Brave looked up at Dylan and wagged his tail in agreement.

"Well then, he's going to need a lot of help from you. So you'd better watch closely—we'll show you." Dylan wasn't sure who she meant by *we* until she called her dog over. "Mustang, come." Mustang hopped to her feet almost before the words were out of Grace's mouth, as if she'd anticipated them. She skipped over to Grace's side and sat down, her front legs together and her eyes locked on Grace. She was waiting for Grace to give her another command. "Good girl," Grace said. "Let's show Dylan and Brave how we do things, okay?"

The dog tipped her head at the sound of Grace's steady, calm voice.

"Mustang—up." Mustang stood up. "Heel." Grace started to walk, and Mustang zipped over, hugged Grace's left side, and fell in step with her. They walked in a big circle. Grace stopped every few feet, and Mustang stopped with her, then started up again as soon as Grace took a step. They stopped, and Grace held out her hand in an upside down fist over Mustang's head. Mustang sat instantly.

Dylan couldn't believe it. Grace hadn't even had to say the word *sit*—she'd just used a hand signal.

"Good." Grace held out an open hand, palm first, toward the dog. Dylan figured out pretty quickly that it must have meant *stay*, because Grace turned around and walked away while Mustang sat patiently, her eyes glued to Grace as she waited for her next command.

It was one of the coolest things Dylan had ever seen. It was almost like Grace and Mustang were telepathic. Could he and Brave be like that one day too?

Grace came over to Dylan, who was holding Brave by the rope collar. He looked down at Brave, who was busy chewing on his own paw, and his heart sank. How would he ever teach Brave anything even close to that in two short weeks? Could Brave ever go from being a wild dog who lived outside, exposed to the elements but totally free, to being an obedient, attentive pet?

Was there any hope at all that they could pull this off?

Grace whistled, and Mustang sprang up and ran to her. She sat down at Grace's feet while Grace rubbed her behind the ears in a way that set her tail wagging.

Dylan stood there with his mouth open. "How do you do that without even speaking out loud?"

"Body language, hand signals. It took some time, but we got to understand each other. Don't worry, you and Brave will get there too."

"I wouldn't even know how to start," Dylan said.

"The trick is exercise, discipline, and affection," Grace said. "First you tire him out a little through exercise. Then you teach him the rules. Then you reward him with food or some good petting and scratching."

Dylan knew that Brave had already gotten plenty of exercise that morning, so he moved on to the discipline portion. He waved a fist over Brave's head, just like Grace had. But Brave didn't sit like Mustang did—he just stood there with his tail wagging, following Dylan's fist with his eyes. Dylan couldn't help but laugh. Clearly Brave had no idea what was going on, and soon he jumped up and started spinning in a circle like he wanted to play a game.

"Don't get ahead of yourself," Grace said. "He doesn't understand what you want yet. You have to break it up into little lessons, just like they do in school. Teach him one small thing at a time."

She showed Dylan how to hold a treat in his hand, which —like the bread from the day before—really got Brave's attention.

"Sit." As he said the word, Dylan patted the dog firmly on the rump while tugging up gently on his collar. When Brave lowered his bottom to the ground—grazing the grass with it more than actually sitting—Dylan gave him the snack. They worked on that a few times, until Brave was pretty consistently following the command.

Then Dylan tried to get the dog to stay. He had Brave sit, then gave the command and backed away step by step. At first Brave chased after Dylan, snuffling at his hand in search of a treat. But after a few tries he realized that Dylan wouldn't give him anything unless he waited, and he started to get the hang of it. Soon they had a new pattern down: If Brave waited for Dylan to call him before moving, he'd get the treat. But if he moved on his own, there was no treat.

They practiced it a dozen times over, and Brave improved each time. Dylan was amazed to watch Brave learning, but he noticed something else about him too. There was a new lightness in the dog's step—he was relaxed but energized. He was happy. And that made Dylan happy too.

Dylan thought back to the day his dad had taught him to ride a bike a few years ago—the way his dad had patiently held the handlebars for balance and waited for Dylan to get up on the seat. Then he'd started walking backwards while Dylan pedaled slowly. Only when his dad sensed it was the right moment did he take his hands away, first for a second, then two, then for several seconds. All the while he talked to Dylan, calmly telling him he could do it.

Dylan had been so excited to learn how to ride his bike, and so proud of himself. But now he realized that it was his dad who'd felt even prouder than he could ever have imagined.

Dylan had never taught anyone like this before, and it made him feel good to know he could do it. But it was even better to see Brave's progress. After an hour of practice, Brave did it perfectly.

"He's tired," Grace said. "Let's let him end on a high note." She and Dylan kneeled down on either side of Brave and gave him a good scratch from head to tail.

By the end of the day, Dylan, Brave, Grace, and Mustang were all covered in dirt and dust. Mr. Garcia called them in from the field, and Dylan followed Grace back to the ranch house, with Brave walking by his side. It seemed like Brave was a little calmer now—and like something had changed between him and Dylan. They were more at ease together, like they had the beginning of an understanding. When Brave got ahead of him, Dylan stopped and waited until Brave noticed and stopped too. Then Dylan would start walking again and Brave would wait for him to catch up, then fall in beside him.

Mr. Garcia was waiting for them on the porch.

"Grace texted me that you did okay for your first day," Mr. Garcia said.

"It wasn't easy," Dylan admitted, wiping his face with his hands and only spreading the dirt and sweat around more.

"Not supposed to be," Mr. Garcia said with a chuckle. "But it sounds like you were a big help to my daughter."

"I'm happy to do it, sir." Dylan's back and legs were aching, and he was ready for a good warm shower, but he was proud that Grace and Mr. Garcia thought he'd done okay.

Then Mr. Garcia reached into his pocket and pulled out a wad of cash, holding it out to Dylan.

"What's this?"

"Your pay for the day," Mr. Garcia said. "A good day's work deserves a good day's pay."

Dylan couldn't mask his surprise. This wasn't part of the deal he'd made with Grace. They were just going to trade work for dog training. "Oh, Mr. Garcia, thank you, but I can't—"

"Sure you can, son," Mr. Garcia said, whacking Dylan on the shoulder so hard that he winced. "I hear you could use the money for a new couch."

Dylan's cheeks burned and he looked down at the ground. "You heard that right," Dylan said. "Thank you, sir."

Like a giant weight was off his chest, Dylan led Brave from the ranch. His whole body was shaking with exhaustion, but in a way that felt new and different and not all bad—like he'd worked hard and earned something good in return. And if he kept earning money, then he could pay his mom back for the couch, plus buy supplies and food for Brave—it was a win-win. He looked down at Brave, who looked back up at him, his tongue hanging out of his mouth.

Dylan wondered if Brave felt it too. He grinned at the dog as they walked side by side in the late-afternoon sun.

★ CHAPTER 12 ★

"Dylan? You understand what the assignment is?"

Dylan heard his name but it took a second for him to realize he should respond. "Yeah—yes, I mean. I got it."

His math teacher, Mr. Shin, looked unconvinced, but the bell rang before he could probe any further.

Dylan snatched up his books and bolted from the classroom. He'd had a hard time concentrating all day—even harder than usual for a Monday. His mind was full of thoughts about Brave and the Garcia Ranch. He'd been so busy doodling pictures of the dog in his notebook that he'd barely heard a word his teachers had said.

Dylan ran through the hall, wishing Brave were there alongside him. In just a couple of short days, he'd gotten used to the feeling of the dog running by his legs. He couldn't wait to get back on the ranch later that day, where they could have some open space and pick up their training where they'd left off. He grabbed his lunch from his locker and hustled to the cafeteria, wondering what he was going to tell Jaxon and the guys about his weekend.

He turned the corner fast and bumped right into Grace. Her lunch bag went flying across the hall, ripping open and spilling its contents across the floor.

"Hey!" she yelped before she saw who it was. "Oh, hi, Dylan. What's up?"

For a second, Dylan was confused by how friendly Grace was. They'd spent so many years at the same school without even acknowledging each other, so it was weird that they'd become friends overnight. They'd spent the entire day working together on the ranch, but it almost seemed like a dream.

"Sorry about your lunch." Dylan kneeled down to pick up a sandwich that had skidded a few feet away.

"No worries," she said. Together they gathered a banana and a granola bar and put them back in the bag as best they could.

Dylan winced as he tried to stand up.

"You sore?" Grace asked with a laugh.

"Not really," Dylan lied. The truth was, he'd had trouble getting out of bed that morning, and he'd needed a good hot shower to get his aching muscles moving. He wanted to change the subject. "I'm just heading to the cafeteria."

"Me too. Want to sit together?"

"Together?" The word popped out of his mouth before he could stop it.

"Yeah, together." Grace grinned at him like he was being ridiculous. "You know, when people sit around the same table and talk to each other. You can meet my friends."

Dylan knew the group she was talking about. The Ranch Kids—that's what Jaxon had started calling them in third grade, and the name had stuck. The Ranch Kids pretty much stayed to themselves, and other kids considered them a little rough around the edges. In other words, they weren't the popular crowd, and the name wasn't exactly a compliment.

He was pretty sure Grace didn't know what Dylan and his buddies called her and her friends. He'd used the name many times over the years without a second thought, but now a wave of guilt washed over him. How could it be occurring to him for the first time that maybe it wasn't very nice to call them that—and maybe Grace and her friends wouldn't like it? How had he been such a dope for so long?

All of this flashed through Dylan's mind while Grace stared at him, waiting for an answer. He shifted back and forth on his feet. He realized with a start that he actually really *wanted* to sit with Grace and her friends, but something was stopping him. A single thought wormed its way into his brain: What would Jaxon say?

Dylan opened his mouth to speak, but no words came out. He couldn't even think of a good excuse.

Grace's face fell, and she pressed her lips into a flat smile. "It's cool," she said. "Go sit with your friends." She clutched her lunch bag to her chest. "I'll see you on the ranch after school."

"Right. Yes—see you there," he said. Grace had set him free, but somehow that only made Dylan feel worse.

He watched her walk to her lunch table and set her stuff down. Her friends started talking to her excitedly, and she joined in their conversation without a glance back at him. Dylan hurried to his usual table with the guys. As he slid into his spot at the end, the guys were staring at him strangely. Dylan's skin prickled. He got the sense that they'd just been talking about him.

"What's up?" he asked.

No one answered. Jaxon sat directly across from him but avoided making eye contact. He took a bite out of his sandwich, chewing slowly while staring down at the table. The rest of the guys were silent. They seemed like they were waiting for something, but Dylan had no idea what.

Finally Jaxon spoke. "Why didn't you text me back last night?" he asked Dylan. "Too busy with that dog?"

Dylan gulped. He'd meant to reply to Jaxon, but he'd gotten so distracted after finishing work and getting Brave home and catching up on his homework. Plus he hadn't had the stomach to watch the video Jaxon had cut together of them throwing the balloons over the bridge.

"Oh, yeah. Sorry—"

"It's cool," Jaxon said, though the tone of his voice made it sound like it was anything but. "So really. What were you up to?"

Dylan's face felt hot. The guys around the table were still staring at him. Why was he suddenly feeling like he was in trouble—like he did when he could tell his mom was mad at him but he wasn't sure why? His gut told him it would be a bad idea to tell his friends the truth about what he'd been doing all weekend. They didn't need to know about how he'd helped Grace and started training Brave. They would never understand.

He scrambled for something—anything—they'd believe. "Dude, my mom grounded me," he blurted out. Getting in trouble was definitely something they could all relate to. "After I came home from throwing water balloons."

The guys nodded. All except Sammy, the joker with curly hair who hung out with Jaxon almost as much as Dylan did.

"Why'd she ground you?" Sammy asked. It sounded more like a challenge than a question.

"I didn't clean my room. She took away my phone and I couldn't leave the house. It was brutal."

Dylan squirmed under Jaxon's steady gaze. Was Jaxon trying to see if he was telling the truth?

"You know how tough my mom is," Dylan said to Jaxon.

After a moment, Jaxon nodded. "That sucks, dude."

Dylan exhaled, relieved that Jaxon seemed to believe him. Once Jaxon had accepted Dylan's story, Sammy and the rest of the crew nodded all around, throwing some pity his way.

"What did you want to tell me, anyway?" Dylan asked, happy to change the subject.

"That slo-mo video I made of us throwing the water balloons?" Jaxon was bursting with pride. "Did you watch it yet?"

Dylan shook his head.

"What?" Jaxon looked genuinely disappointed. "Oh right —your mom had your phone. It's so cool—somebody pull it up on YouTube and show him!" The other kids scrambled for their phones.

"YouTube?" Dylan said. He swallowed hard. Dropping water balloons onto unsuspecting cars hadn't felt exactly right—or legal—and Dylan was surprised that Jaxon had gone through with posting the stunt online, where anyone could see it. Wouldn't that lead straight to trouble?

Their friend Bowie pulled out his phone and his eyes went wide. "Jax! You've got five thousand two hundred twenty-four hits!"

Jaxon let out a whoop and raised his arms in triumph. "Epic. Told you so."

Dylan's stomach wriggled as he watched the video. It was an instant classic—the balloons blowing to smithereens in slow motion.

"Now play it at regular speed—Dyl, you won't believe how fast they hit," Jaxon said.

Bowie started the video again. This time the balloons were a blur onscreen, and they landed with a *Whap! Whap! Whap!* Dylan started at the sound. It was familiar, but it took him a second to place it. The exploding balloons sounded like fireworks going off—and he couldn't imagine what they sounded like from inside the cars.

Dylan watched his friends cheer and high-five each other, and out of the corner of his eye he saw the cafeteria monitor shooting them a stern look.

There was something about the whole situation that made him feel a little queasy.

He felt Jaxon's eyes on him, and he turned to see a strange look on his friend's face.

"What's the matter?" Jaxon asked. "You don't look psyched."

"Nah, of course I am," Dylan fumbled. "Are you gonna do it again?"

"Maybe." Jaxon shrugged.

"Do it! Do it!" the group chanted.

"Okay, you convinced me." Jaxon smirked. The cafeteria monitor started toward them, and Jaxon quickly shushed the table. He waited for the monitor to move away before whispering, "We're definitely doing it again. But this time I want to make it even bigger and better—and even more dangerous."

Dylan's blood went cold, but he didn't say anything.

"It'll be beyond cool," Jaxon said. "Everyone around after school today? We can start getting supplies."

The group nodded enthusiastically. Dylan nodded too, hoping no one could see on his face that he was faking it. He was racking his brain for any reason to get out of joining them when he realized he actually couldn't go—he had to be at the ranch after school. There was no way he was telling Jaxon that, though.

"Oh, bummer—" Dylan started to say.

"Don't even tell me—" Jaxon interrupted him.

"I'm still grounded," Dylan lied. He hated doing it, but he thought of Brave and knew it was the right thing to do.

"Dude, your mom sucks."

"It's not her fault. It's mine for not doing my chores."

"Correction then. You suck."

Dylan looked down, stung by Jaxon's words.

"Oh well," Jaxon said with a laugh, looking around at the other guys. "We're doing it with or without you."

The guys at the table cheered, and the cafeteria monitor threw them another dirty look. But this time, they didn't even seem to care.

Dylan felt strange, like he was watching the scene from above. He was sitting next to his best friend, at the same table they sat at every day, but he suddenly felt like he was on the outside. While the other guys were watching the balloon video again, he scarfed down the sandwich his mom had made. When he was sure Jaxon wasn't looking, Dylan glanced across the cafeteria at Grace sitting with her friends. One of them was up on his feet, acting out a funny story while the others cracked up.

Dylan wondered what the kid was saying. Maybe he'd ask Grace later. His friends hooted and hollered as the video ended, and Grace looked up at the sound of the commotion. She caught Dylan's eye, and he gave her a small wave and smile. She nodded in return and turned back to her friends.

Dylan cringed and wondered if Grace was mad at him for not wanting to sit with her. He wished she hadn't looked away so fast—he would just have to apologize to her later. He couldn't wait for school to end so he could get Brave and head over to the Garcias'. On the other hand, he felt bad about lying to Jaxon and the guys. And he was worried: Was Jaxon going to try to pressure him into making another video? There was only so long he could pretend that he was grounded.

As the bell signaled the end of lunch and the start of sixth period, Dylan wondered how much worse he could feel.

★ CHAPTER 13 ★

"How long have you and Jaxon been friends?" Grace dropped an armful of branches onto the growing pile. She turned and looked out over the field they were clearing, watching Brave and Mustang chase each other.

"Forever," Dylan replied. "I don't remember not being friends with him." He tossed a spiny jumble of tree limbs onto the pile and shook out his arms.

"That might explain it," Grace said under her breath.

"Huh?"

She turned to look at him. "I'm just not sure why you're so tight with him, that's all."

Dylan wasn't sure how to respond. It hadn't occurred to him that if he had noticed that Jaxon had been acting differently, maybe other people had too. But hearing someone else talk about him suddenly made Dylan feel protective of his oldest friend.

"Jaxon's cool," he said.

Grace raised an eyebrow and tipped her head to the side.

"He's not that bad . . ." Dylan trailed off. The words sounded hollow out loud. "He just likes to have fun, that's all."

Grace let out a snort. "Yeah, but at whose expense?"

Dylan wanted to argue with her, but he thought back to the excited look on Jaxon's face as the water balloons arced through the air and smashed into the cars below. Grace was right.

"Sorry," Grace said. "I know he's your friend. I don't mean to sound harsh."

"It's fine," Dylan said.

"I just—" Grace paused, as if she were deciding whether or not to say what she was thinking.

"What?"

"It's just—well, you seem like a better person than that. I mean, you're nice and you don't act like you're better than anyone else."

Her words made Dylan feel two distinctly different things at once: squirmy from the compliment, and bummed for Jaxon. Did accepting the one also mean accepting the other?

"Thanks?" As soon as he said it, Dylan felt a pang of guilt. Was it still his job to defend his friend if Grace was right about him? Maybe he was supposed to convince Grace that Jaxon wasn't so bad — that he was just going through a phase. But then Dylan thought about how it would feel to have a water balloon explode on your car out of nowhere. The sound alone would make anyone jump out of their skin.

The sound.

That reminded him of something — and he was relieved to have a reason to change the subject.

"You know," he said, "I was thinking about what happens when Brave freaks out."

Grace seemed happy to drop the Jaxon topic too. "Yeah? What'd you come up with?"

"It seems like he's mostly freaked out by really loud sounds."

"Which makes sense," Grace said. "I mean, the hurricane was so loud."

They both shuddered at the memory.

"And right before he ran out of my house and came to the ranch," Dylan went on, "it sounded like fireworks were going off or something."

"And when we dropped the tree trunk," Grace said with a nod, "it was loud."

"Exactly."

"So maybe if we can help him learn not to be scared by sounds," Dylan said, "he'll get better overall."

"Good thinking," Grace said.

"How do we help him do that, though?"

She thought for a second. "When my little brother was born, my dad kept telling the rest of us *not* to be quiet around the house."

"What do you mean?"

"I mean, he told us it was okay to watch TV at full volume and run the vacuum cleaner and do all the usual stuff because the baby had to get used to the noise."

"So, you're saying we should expose Brave to lots of noise to help him get over his fear of . . . noise?"

"That's exactly what I'm saying."

Dylan considered the idea for a second and shrugged. "Let's give it a try."

Grace checked the time on her phone. "We can get started right now. I have to get Rey out for some exercise anyway."

"Who?"

"Rey. My horse."

"Your horse's name is Ray?"

"Yeah, but with an *e*," Grace said. "Like *el rey*. It means 'the king' in Spanish. And he's loud. Well, his hooves are anyway."

Dylan remembered the sight of Brave trapped between the bucking bull and the horse's stomping hooves the first time they'd come to the ranch. He didn't want that to happen again—and he was pretty sure Brave didn't either. "Are you sure that's a good place to start? What if Brave flips out again?"

"It'll be okay—it'll just be me and Rey, and I can control him. Plus, if Brave is going to keep hanging out on the ranch, he has to get used to horses sooner rather than later. Horses and dogs are a team around here. Come on." Grace turned and started walking back toward the barn and corral. She let out one sharp whistle and Mustang came racing across the field to follow her. Brave followed Mustang, tromping happily through the grass.

It sounded risky, but Dylan trusted Grace. He'd seen how well she could handle her horse, and it was clear that Mustang was an amazingly well-trained dog. If this was the way to help Brave, then that's what they would do.

★ ★ ★

"Aaaaand stop," Grace said. "Right there."

Dylan and Brave came to a halt at the center of the ring. He held the dog by an old leash of Mustang's that Grace had given them. Brave walked close by his side and sat down as soon as Dylan gave him the command.

"Good boy," Dylan said, patting Brave on the head. "Now what?" he asked Grace.

"Now I'm going to get on Rey and you're going to keep Brave close to you."

"Okay." Dylan gripped Brave's leash tightly.

"Remember," Grace said, "positive reinforcement."

"Positive reinforcement. Got it," Dylan said.

Grace disappeared into the barn and a moment later returned atop her horse, a statuesque white Arabian. She began to walk him slowly around the ring. The clip-clop of his hooves on the dirt was even and faint.

Brave's ears sprang up and back, and his tail shot straight out behind him, curling up at the very tip. His eyes were locked on the horse, and a line of fur stood up on his back —but he stayed calm.

"Good boy," Dylan said. He pulled a treat out of his pocket and held it under Brave's nose. Without taking his eyes off the horse, Brave took the bit of food gently in his teeth and chewed it once before swallowing it.

Grace dug her heels into Rey's side and clucked her tongue. The horse picked up speed, moving at a quick trot. As the sound of his hooves got louder, Brave grew agitated. He whined and began to pant, and Dylan could see his chest moving up and down as he breathed quickly. Brave lifted and lowered his front paws in a nervous dance.

Dylan shortened the slack on the leash. "It's okay, boy,"

he said soothingly. "It's just Grace and Rey." Brave let out a little whimper but stayed put. *So far so good*, Dylan thought.

Grace and Rey reached the far end of the corral and came around in a wide circle, heading back toward Dylan and Brave.

"Sit," Dylan said, preparing the dog. At first Brave ignored him, but Dylan tugged gently on the leash, and the dog, looking uneasy, did as he was told. "Good boy." Dylan held out another treat, but this time Brave was too distracted to care about it.

The sound of Rey's footsteps pounding on the dirt grew louder and louder as the horse approached them. Dylan looked down. The dog was shaking. Grace and the horse passed by, and the noise was at its peak. As Rey's hooves came down, the ground vibrated beneath their feet.

Brave couldn't take it anymore. Frightened, he hopped to his feet and tried to run—but he was attached to a leash for possibly the first time in his life. The leash snapped tight and yanked Dylan's arm, hard, nearly pulling him off his feet. Brave cried out in pain and surprise as Dylan leaned back, trying to stay upright. Brave dug at the dirt, desperate to break free and get away.

"Brave! Stop!" Dylan shouted. His shoulder was burning, and he held on to the leash with both hands, taking a step backward to restrain the dog.

Grace pulled up on the reins and brought Rey to a full stop. She hopped down and ran over to help Dylan with Brave.

"Easy, boy," she cooed as she approached. "It's okay, Brave. It's just me." She kneeled down in front of Brave and sat there, not touching him or giving him any commands —just reassuring him with her presence and her voice.

Slowly, Brave began to calm down, and his body started to relax. Dylan exhaled and exchanged a relieved look with Grace. He lowered his arms and loosened his grip on the leash, opening and closing his hands to get the blood flowing back into them. Brave was still on high alert, but his breathing slowed and his fur came down.

Until Rey got antsy.

Behind Grace, Rey snorted loudly and stomped his foot, then let out a shrill—and booming—whinny. All at the same instant, Grace's head whipped around toward the sound, Brave splayed his legs and lowered his body to the ground in a defensive posture, and Dylan shouted "No!" Then, just as Dylan's reflexes kicked in to tighten his grip on the leash, he felt it slip through his fingers, and Brave was gone.

The dog was a blue-gray blur. He shot toward Rey, but the horse raised one large hoof in the air as Brave came close. Brave turned on a dime, zigzagging in another direction, not losing a bit of speed.

"Brave—stop!" Dylan called out. But it was too late. Brave ducked under the lower rung of the fence and disappeared around the barn in a flash. "I'll get him," Dylan said to Grace.

Deflated, he set out after the dog. He searched under trucks, behind tractors, even in Rey's empty stall. After ten solid minutes of searching, he heard a gentle rustling behind a bale of hay in the back corner of the barn. Dylan sat down on the blocky rectangle and peered over it at the dog, who quivered behind it.

"Hey, bub."

Brave looked up at him, his yellow-orange eyes big, round, and sad.

"It's okay, Brave. I get it. Rey's a big horse—he scares me, too."

Brave whimpered in agreement and swatted at the hay with one paw. Dylan reached over and scratched the top of Brave's head. After a minute, he swung his legs over and lowered himself onto the ground next to Brave. The dog put his front paws on Dylan's lap and lowered his head onto them. They sat like that, tucked into the corner of the barn with Brave half lying across Dylan's legs and Dylan running a hand along Brave's short, silky coat.

"Dylan?" Grace called out. "Where are you?"

"Back here," he responded. After a second, Grace stared down at them over the hay bale. "Hey," Dylan said.

"Uh, hey." She shot him a quizzical look. "You two comfortable back there?"

Dylan smiled and ran his thumb along the dip between Brave's eyes, where his fur was the softest. "Yep. We sure are."

"Well, I hate to break up the snuggling, but he has to get back out there."

"Hasn't he had enough for today?" Dylan asked. He wasn't going to say it out loud, but he'd had enough too.

"Never end a training session on a negative note," Grace explained. "We're going to do it again, and we'll stop when he's calm and doing a good job."

Dylan sighed. "Okay. Fine." He gently nudged Brave off his lap and stood up, brushing hay off his chaps. Brave stood up and shook himself out with a loud flap of his ears. "Come on, boy. One more time."

Much to Dylan's surprise, it wasn't one more time. It was two, then three. Brave wasn't thrilled about the horse, but he seemed to have gotten something out of his system. Each time Rey went by, the dog was a little less skittish.

On Rey's last pass around the ring, Brave watched him go by nonchalantly. Finally he lay down in the middle of the ring, rolled onto his side, raised his front paw to his mouth, and began cleaning it.

"Looks like he's getting used to it," Grace said, hopping

off the horse and walking over to them. "He's a quick learner, Brave."

"He's brilliant," Dylan beamed, his chest bursting with pride. He looked over at Grace and was flooded with appreciation for his new friend. She was the only shot he had at keeping Brave, and Dylan knew it. "Thanks, Grace," he said.

"You're welcome. Brave's a good dog—I hope you can keep him."

At the sound of his name, Brave scrambled to his feet, plunked his rump down on the ground in a perfect sit, raised his ears, and locked his gaze on Dylan. There was a desperate *I'm such a good boy* look in his eye.

"I think he's figured out how to get a treat." Dylan laughed.

"Like I said, he's a quick learner." Grace looked from Dylan to Brave and back again. She seemed to be thinking about something.

"What?" Dylan asked cautiously.

"I think you should try it."

"Uh . . . try what?"

"Riding Rey."

"Riding what?"

"Rey. The horse."

"I know who Rey is. I just don't know if I want to ride him." As if in response, Rey squinted suspiciously at Dylan.

"Why not? You'll never meet a sweeter or calmer horse. Brave's doing great—now it's your turn to try something new."

Dylan laughed, waiting for Grace to say she was kidding. But she held him with a steady, if slightly amused, gaze.

"Go on," she said. "Saddle up, cowboy."

So far, everything Grace had said or done had been right. She had taught Brave more in a couple of days than Dylan could have hoped to teach him in a month. And, if he was being honest with himself, she'd taught Dylan just as much.

He threw up his hands.

"Fine," he said. "But I've never ridden a horse before—so don't say I didn't warn you."

★ CHAPTER 14 ★

Dylan looked straight down. Way, way down. His vision swooped and he gripped the horn on the saddle tightly. He sat uncomfortably atop Rey, amazed at the hardness of the leather seat—and how high off the ground he was.

"Stop being so nervous," Grace said as she adjusted the strap on the stirrups. "Rey can tell. You're stressing him out."

"Easy for you to say," Dylan shot back. "You've probably been riding horses since you were a baby."

She thought about that for a second. "Yeah." She shrugged. "I guess I have been."

The horse exhaled sharply and stomped his feet, unhappy to have an inexperienced rider on his back. Dylan sucked in his breath.

"Steady there," Grace said. She held the reins tightly and stroked Rey's muzzle to calm him down.

"When you see someone riding a horse, they don't seem

like they're this high up," Dylan said, trying to hide the nerves in his voice.

"Yup," Grace said. "It takes some getting used to. Just stay calm and confident, and he'll feel your energy and respond to you."

Dylan took a deep breath and tried to do as she said —but how was he supposed to stay calm when he felt like he was twenty feet off the ground? He looked over at Brave, who was not-so-happily tied to the fence across the corral. Brave had made incredible progress, but Dylan and Grace had agreed that it would be best to keep him out of the way while Dylan was learning to ride. If Dylan got nervous, Brave could really freak out—while Dylan was on top of a giant horse.

Brave whined at him from afar. He was still not used to being restrained, and he wasn't afraid to let everyone know how he felt about the new turn of events.

"I've been sitting up here for a while," Dylan said. "When do I stop sitting and start riding?"

Grace smiled. "Sounds like you're ready to try a walk."

"As ready as I'll ever be," Dylan said. He couldn't believe that just a few days ago he'd been playing video games with Jaxon, and now he was dressed in cowboy duds sitting on a horse. It didn't feel real.

Grace handed over the reins. "Keep a light grip, but let Rey know you're there."

"I don't know what that means." Dylan's heart was pounding.

"You will," Grace said. "And remember—patience, persistence, and consistency. You're the boss."

The horse snorted as he sensed the passing of the reins. He took one lumbering step backward, unsure of what to do. Dylan yanked the reins in response.

"Careful—it's not a brake," Grace explained. "Start out a little snug on the reins but don't yank. Use your legs to tell him what you want him to do."

Again, Dylan understood the words but not the message. There was only one way to figure it out, though—and that was by trying it. Dylan exhaled slowly, closed his eyes for a moment, then reopened them. He gathered the reins until he felt light contact with the bit in Rey's mouth, then he squeezed lightly with his lower legs like Grace had taught him. This was Rey's cue to walk forward.

At first the horse didn't move. Frustration rose in Dylan's chest, but he heard Grace's instructions in his head. This was what she had meant by persistence, he guessed. Not to mention patience.

He kept up the pressure with his calves until the horse

took a few rocking steps forward, just like Grace had said he would.

But no sooner had Rey started to move than Dylan began to panic. Now not only was he high off the ground, but he also felt off-balance and precarious—and like he was struggling to keep himself in the saddle. Grace had warned him it would feel rough at first and given him some tips on how to handle it. Now that the horse was moving, though, Dylan seemed unable to recall—let alone follow—her simple directions.

"Remember—face forward and keep your body relaxed," Grace coached him from the side. That sounded nearly impossible to Dylan. Riding a horse was like trying to remember a dozen things at the same time, and by the time he remembered one, he'd forgotten all the others.

As Rey walked, Dylan rocked front to back and side to side. Fighting to stay in the saddle, he reflexively squeezed Rey's sides with his legs—which the horse just took as a cue to go faster. Suddenly the horse was trotting, and Dylan was bouncing up and down on the saddle so hard, it felt like his brain was rattling and someone was kicking him in the rear over and over again.

"How's it feel?" Grace asked.

"Feels g-g-good," Dylan said, his teeth knocking together.

Riding looked so easy when he saw Grace and the other cowboys do it, but now he knew how hard they must have worked to get that good. He didn't know how Grace rode so gracefully when he felt like a circus clown doing slapstick.

Brave barked at him from across the ring.

"Don't worry, Brave," Dylan called out to the dog. "I'm going to survive this." Dylan wanted nothing more than to get off the horse, shake out his legs, and walk away before anyone got hurt. But he reminded himself that if Brave could learn something new, so could he. They were in this together.

"Stay with it now," Grace said. "Don't give up."

Dylan took a couple of deep breaths, feeling his pulse throbbing in his neck.

"Look up," Grace said. "Look where you want to go, not at the back of Rey's head."

Dylan realized he'd been staring at Rey's mane, trying to steady himself. He exhaled slowly and looked up—only to realize that the horse was heading straight for the fence.

Dylan panicked. What if Rey didn't stop? Where were the brakes on this horse?

"Turn him!" Grace shouted.

Dylan's mind went blank. How was he supposed to do that?! Blood pounded in his ears and then, as if someone had turned down the volume, the world went quiet. He was watching himself on a silent film, moving steadily toward the fence. *Would Rey crash into it or jump over it?* he found himself wondering. And which was worse?

Brave let out a loud series of barks so intense it startled Dylan back into himself. The fence was just a few feet away when, in a flash, he remembered how to turn. Dylan gently pulled the reins back with his left hand while applying pressure with his left leg. Sure enough, the horse responded, turning around Dylan's left leg just like Grace had described. In an instant, they were out of danger and riding parallel to the fence.

"Yee-ha!" Dylan shouted. "Did you see that!?"

"Nice!" Grace called out. "You're getting it!"

Even Brave could tell that something had changed, and his cries shifted from fear to excitement. He yipped and pawed at the ground.

Now that he realized he could guide the horse, Dylan started to enjoy himself. His tensed muscles relaxed, and he sensed how to stay upright in the saddle without sending the wrong cues to the horse. It wasn't like talking to Brave exactly, but it was similar in some ways. Dylan had to take charge—he had to stay calm, make simple commands, then give the animal a chance to respond. If he got frustrated or rushed, the horse would get confused and either stop responding altogether or, worse, do something unpredictable.

Dylan turned the horse again and headed back toward Grace. He saw the excitement on her face and it struck him: He was really riding a horse. Dylan couldn't help it—he sat a little taller in the saddle.

"Let's give Brave a chance to get in the game," Grace said. She unhooked Brave's leash from the fence but held on to it loosely. "See if you can get him to sit and stay from up there."

For a second, Dylan's brain got scrambled as he tried to sort out the different commands he would need to give his legs, arms, eyes, mouth, and dog. Then he took a breath and called out to Brave. "Sit!" he said confidently.

Brave quieted down but stood exactly where he was, watching Dylan and Rey, his tail wagging.

"Sit," Dylan called out again. Still nothing. He twisted his upper body to the right ever so slightly so he could see Brave better. When he did, he pulled his right leg in without realizing it, applying pressure to Rey's side. Suddenly, Rey took a sharp turn and picked up speed—headed straight for Brave.

Brave's tail stopped wagging and dipped between his legs. His ears went back, and a low, steady growl emanated from his throat.

"Stop!" Dylan said to the horse, but he'd forgotten the

actual command or movement or whatever he was supposed to do. He looked up and saw Brave's amber eyes go wide with panic. The dog tugged hard on his leash, and Grace held him steady with both hands.

"Squeeze with both legs—your whole legs!" she called out to Dylan. "And pull back—but not too hard or he'll buck."

As Brave snarled, Dylan frantically tried to execute the series of steps Grace was giving him. His heart was beating hard in his chest, but somehow he managed to get Rey to come to a full stop. They were just a couple of feet from the dog, who let out one final yelp.

"Nice!" Grace said. She stepped over and patted Rey on the neck. The horse sputtered and toyed with the bit in his mouth.

Dylan let out a nervous, relieved laugh and adjusted the cowboy hat on his head. "That was terrifying," he said. "But also kind of cool."

"I knew you'd like it up there," Grace said.

Dylan looked down at Brave, who also seemed relieved now that the horse wasn't coming right at him. Brave stood up on his hind legs and waved a paw at Dylan.

"Now you know what they say," Grace said. "You've got to get back on the horse."

"I'm still on the horse," Dylan replied.

"Cute. I mean try again."

He sighed. "No breaks on the Garcia Ranch, huh?"

"Nope." Grace shook her head. "Go."

Dylan steered Rey back out into the ring. Now that he knew he could stop—and stop under pressure—he felt more confident in the saddle, like he and Rey had reached some kind of understanding. And sure enough, the more comfortable Dylan felt, the more easily Rey responded to his movements.

When Dylan and Rey had circled around the ring again, he called out to Brave. "Sit!" Dylan wasn't sure how to describe it, but something in his voice sounded different to his own ear. He'd said the same word, but he'd somehow said it in a new way—with more conviction. Brave sensed it too. As soon as the word rang out across the corral, Brave sat.

"Stay," Dylan said. Brave didn't budge. Dylan nudged Rey with his heels and the horse broke into a trot. Dylan wobbled on the saddle but held on as they picked up speed, moving around the circle with a loud clopping sound.

Brave didn't move. He watched Dylan and the horse intently, pulling a little against his leash as they went by.

"Change it up a little with Brave," Grace suggested.

Dylan pulled the horse to a stop. Brave wanted Dylan's attention—he ducked his head and scratched at the ground with one paw. Dylan made eye contact with the dog and waited until he was calm.

"Brave," he said, "come."

Grace let go of the leash as Brave dashed straight toward Dylan, stopping a few feet from Rey.

"Sit."

Brave sat.

"Stay." Dylan rode Rey about ten feet away. Brave watched him go, a longing look in his eye. "Good boy. Come!" Brave ran over to him and sat down by the horse's feet.

Brave was closer to the horse than he'd ever been — and totally calm about it. At that moment, Dylan began to understand that it wasn't about one perfectly spoken command to the dog or one just-right tug on Rey's reins. It was about more than learning the mechanics of how to train or ride an animal. He and Brave were building a true bond.

Brave, who had definitely been through some tough experiences in his short life, was growing to trust Dylan. And that was worth all the hard work in the world.

★ CHAPTER 15 ★

Dylan was bone tired by the time he arrived home, and his body was sore in places he never even knew he had. He walked into the house with Brave by his side, the two of them taking over the mud room as they took off their dirt-streaked gear. Dylan slipped Brave's bandanna over his head and scratched him under the collar. Brave closed his eyes and let out a happy snort.

Dylan's mom passed by the door. "How did it go— Whoa, you look like cowboys!"

Dylan smiled appreciatively. "This cowboy is exhausted," he said. "And starving."

"That's good, because I have a big dinner planned. Chicken-fried steak and sweet potato fries."

"My favorite," Dylan said. Brave let out a hungry bark, perhaps because he could smell the fry oil coming to temperature in the kitchen. Dylan's mom only made chicken-fried steak on special occasions. "What for?"

"Can't a mom make her favorite son his favorite meal?"

"I'm your only son," Dylan said. "But sure. I won't say no."

"The truth is that I'm proud of you, that's all," his mom said, pulling him into a hug. "You've been working really hard to hold up your end of the Brave bargain."

"It's been a lot of work," Dylan admitted. "But fun, too."

His mom pulled away and wrinkled her nose. "Smells like a lot of work. Why don't you go get cleaned up while I get dinner on the table."

Dylan wanted to stay in the hot shower forever, but the scent of dinner lured him back downstairs. As he reached the kitchen doorway, he heard his mom's voice and paused just outside the room to listen. He peeked in and saw Brave sitting by her knee as she stood at the counter, observing her every move.

"You're waiting for me to drop something, I know," she chatted cheerfully to the dog. "But I'm onto you, dog." She reached down and patted the top of his head, and Brave sniffed her palm. "So were you a good boy today?" Brave opened his mouth and yawped at her. "That's what I thought." She pulled plates down from the cabinet. "Do me a favor and set the table, Brave."

"We'll work on that next," Dylan said, stepping into the room and taking the plates from her. "He's a quick learner."

"That's what he was just telling me," his mom said.

Dylan couldn't help noticing how nice it felt to see his mom happy instead of irritated. Over on the table, her phone vibrated and sang a little tune.

"That's your dad," she said. "Can you grab it?"

Dylan swiped at the screen, and after a short delay, a video window popped up.

"Hi, Dad!" He sat down at the table and held the phone in both hands.

"Hey, bud! Good to see your face."

"Good to see your face too."

Brave jumped up and stuffed his face under Dylan's arm and into the frame, curious to see who Dylan was talking to.

"Hey there, mister," Dylan's dad laughed.

"Brave, say hi to Dad."

Brave ran his nose over the screen.

"Okay, okay, you've had your sniffs. Now it's my turn to talk to him," Dylan said to the dog. "Brave, off." He pointed at the floor, and the dog put all four paws back down.

"Nice," his dad said. "He's really responding to you, huh?"

"Dylan was just about to tell me how it went today," his mom said, putting the food on the table and sitting down next to him. She gave her husband a little wave.

"It was incredible," Dylan told his parents. "I rode Rey—that's Grace's horse—"

"You did what!" His mom's jaw dropped open. "I'm sorry I wasn't there to see it."

"Me too," his dad chuckled. "I'd pay good money to see you on a horse, kiddo."

"It was super cool," Dylan went on, his words starting to spill out in a rush. "I mean, not at first—at first it kind of sucked, but I got better at it and learned how to steer him. And Grace was amazing—she helped us so much. We think Brave's scared of loud noises, so she figured out what to do about that. And look at this." Dylan reached into his pocket and took out the cash that Mr. Garcia had given him for the day's work. "If I add this to the money I've already made to pay for the couch and for Brave—"

"Wait, Dyl. Rewind for a second," his mom said. "What was that about Brave being scared of loud noises?"

His parents exchanged a look. "That doesn't sound normal, does it?" his dad asked.

Dylan knew he had to answer carefully. He didn't want to lie to his parents, but he didn't want them to think there was anything really wrong with Brave either. "We think it could be because of the hurricane. Like maybe he was outside while it was happening."

His mom considered that for a moment. "That would

explain it. But is that something that can be fixed in a dog?"

"Grace thinks so. We started trying to get him used to noise, like the horses on the ranch. He did great."

"You two are really dedicated to this, huh?" his dad said.

"We are. He's such an amazing dog—we just want him to be okay." Dylan regretted the words as soon as they came out of his mouth. The air in the room changed, and Dylan held his breath.

"Dyl . . ." His dad shook his head and looked off camera for a second. "We understand that, but if you're not even sure the dog is *okay*, then I don't know."

"He's totally okay!" Dylan jumped in. "Really—he's fine."

"I want to believe you," his dad said with a sigh. "But just remember that taking care of a rescue dog like Brave is a lot of work."

"Right. I know, Dad. And I promise I can do it." Dylan fumbled for the right words. "And I want Brave to be better than okay. I want him to be as *great* as we know he can be."

"We know you do, Dyl," his mom said. "You said you were committed to this and you have been."

"And you're still keeping up with your homework and everything?" his dad asked.

"I am." Dylan nodded for emphasis. "I'm really trying, guys."

His dad had a funny look on his face that Dylan couldn't place at first. He was sort of smiling, and his eyes crinkled up at the sides.

And that's when it hit Dylan—his dad was proud of him. He looked from his dad, framed on the tiny phone screen, to his mom, who sat right next to him, and felt his chest swell. He loved when it felt like they were all together —even if it was just for a few minutes.

And now that Brave was there too, sitting by Dylan's knee, their family felt so complete.

Dylan and his mom ate while they chatted with his dad. The whole time, Brave's ears were up and forward and his eyes were locked on Dylan's plate as he waited not so patiently for a bite. Dylan shook his head at the dog and silently jerked a thumb toward the living room, willing him to go away and not look like a beggar. Brave just stared at him and swept his tail back and forth across the kitchen floor.

"He does seem like a sweet dog," Dylan's dad said.

"Even though he's got terrible table manners," his mom piped in. "Do we have enough dog food for him?"

"We could use some more, actually." Dylan sensed an opportunity. "And I was thinking, maybe I could use some of the money I made to buy him a toy, too?"

As if he recognized the word "toy" and knew who he had to convince, Brave turned his attention to Dylan's mom. He looked up at her with a glint in his big amber eyes, tipped his head to the side, and let out a little yowl. He was going for maximum cuteness.

"You are a handsome fellow, aren't you," she said, reaching out to stroke Brave's head. "And your fur is really soft." She sat back in her chair. "Okay, you two. Let's clean up the dishes and run to the pet store before they close." She turned to the phone. "We'll call you later, sweetie."

"Over and out," Dylan's dad said. "Love you two."

"Love you, Dad. Miss you."

"Miss you too, pal. Bye." The screen went black.

Dylan hopped out of his seat and wrapped his mom in a huge hug. "Thanks, Mom."

"You're welcome." She laughed into his shoulder. "Is this what I have to do to get a hug around here?"

"Yup." Dylan squeezed her harder.

★ ★ ★

The pet store was cavernous and bright, and dogs casually strolled the aisles alongside their people. Brave, on the other hand, was practically beside himself with excitement. His tongue hung out of his mouth, and his entire back half swung left to right as his tail wagged as steadily as a windshield wiper. He hopped up on every shelf, sniffing to take in the thousands of new smells, then exhaling sharply to clear his nostrils so he could sniff again.

"Easy, Brave," Dylan said, shortening the slack on the leash so Brave couldn't jump up as easily. Brave looked over his shoulder at Dylan, as if to say *Seriously? This is the coolest place I've ever seen and you want me to take it easy?* But the dog seemed to settle down.

"He listens to you," Dylan's mom said.

Dylan took that as a good sign. *Keep it up, Brave,* he thought, sending the dog a silent message.

They filled their cart with a big bag of kibble, two stainless steel bowls for water and food, and some high-value training treats. To replace the things Grace had loaned them, Dylan picked out a red collar that would look great on Brave's dark fur, and a new leash that felt like a horse's reins in his hand. Brave watched everything go into the basket, his eyes alight with anticipation. Finally they came to the toy aisle.

"All right, pal, this'll be fun," Dylan said. "Sit." Brave hesitated, distracted by the rows of brightly colored balls and ropes and flying discs and stuffed animals in the shape of squirrels, raccoons, and even a teddy bear. It was overwhelming.

Dylan waited a moment to give Brave a chance to respond, then repeated the command and held out an upside-down closed fist over his head. Brave sat. Dylan's mom nodded, impressed.

"Stay," Dylan said, holding out a palm to Brave. "I'll show you a few things, and you pick, okay?" Brave's ears flicked. "Good."

Dylan grabbed a tough leather hedgehog, a spiky rubber ball, and a long braided rope in a rainbow of colors. He held each one in front of Brave's nose while the dog sniffed and snorted, eyeballed, and even — when no other customers were looking, thankfully — tasted them.

Brave seemed equally thrilled by all of them, so Dylan tried again with a double-handled tug-of-war toy and a squeaky rabbit. When Brave still couldn't decide, Dylan held them all up again, one after the other. When he got to the hedgehog, Brave hopped up on his back legs and put his paws on Dylan's arm. He let out a high-pitched yip.

"Hedgehog for the win!" Dylan's mom laughed.

"Good call, Brave." Dylan hung all the other toys back on their pegs. He held the hedgehog in his hand as they made their way to the register, but Brave kept jumping up on him impatiently. Finally, Dylan pulled off the tag and gave it to him to carry.

Dylan used his cash to pay for everything, and the three of them headed for the parking lot. Brave walked with his head up, gently holding his new, precious toy in his mouth.

A little girl riding in a cart pointed at Brave as she passed.

"Look, Daddy!" She giggled. "That pretty dog is carrying a toy all by himself!"

"He sure is," the dad replied. "What a good dog."

Dylan's mom squeezed his shoulder, and Dylan beamed with pride.

★ CHAPTER 16 ★

Three more days.

That's how long they had before the two weeks was up. That's how long Dylan had to convince his mom to let him keep Brave.

If Brave wasn't well trained enough in three days, he would have to go back to the shelter. The good news was that so far, no one had gone there looking for him. But the bad news was that if Dylan couldn't keep him . . . there might be no one else to adopt Brave, and then there was no telling what would happen to him.

Dylan had been spending as much time as possible on the ranch, hoping to put Brave's training into overdrive. He and Grace had been working hard, in every sense of the word. Day after day, they'd spent long afternoons hauling debris, digging holes for new fenceposts, and taking turns riding Rey. During all of that, they were constantly training Brave, who was working pretty hard himself.

Every evening, Dylan had come home wiped out—and happier than he'd ever been. As the field cleared and the pile of dead branches grew, or the line of freshly dug post holes stretched farther and farther, it was amazing to see the immediate results of their labor.

The same thing was happening with Brave. As they trained every day for hours, it was clear that something had changed between them. It was like they were communicating on a whole different frequency—with words and without. Like Brave knew what Dylan wanted him to do before he said a command out loud or gave a hand signal. Brave was attuned to Dylan in a whole new way, and he had become an incredibly calm and well-behaved dog.

That was, in every way but one.

No matter how hard Dylan and Grace tried, no matter what they did to help him, they couldn't totally get Brave past his fear of loud sounds. The dog was making some progress. He could sit quietly in the ring while Rey galloped around him in circles. He didn't bat an eyelash when Dylan or Grace dumped a heavy tree trunk onto the stack of splintered branches in the field. But those were things Brave had gotten used to—they were familiar. The second something unexpected came up, like a truckload of steel rods being delivered to the barn, or a digger clanging down the ranch road, it was another story.

When that happened, Brave still cowered like the lost dog Dylan had found that first day, shivering behind a dumpster.

Dylan wiped his sweaty brow on his shirt and dusted off his work gloves. He stooped down to pick up the shovel and jammed it into the dry dirt. Then he put one cowboy-booted foot down on top of it, pressed it down farther, and scooped out a shovelful of earth. He tossed it onto the mound to his left. As if the spray of dirt were a squeaky toy, Brave and Mustang dove after it. When they couldn't catch it in their mouths, they dropped to their bellies and rolled around in it.

"Brave! Mustang!" Dylan said. "Cut it out you guys are filthy!" The dogs responded by chasing each other up and over the dirt pile and across the field, toward the spot where Grace was chugging from a bottle of water. They tackled each other near her feet, and she jumped out of the way with a laugh.

Grace hoisted her shovel over her shoulder and walked over to Dylan. They stood side by side watching the dogs as the sun dropped lower in the late-afternoon sky.

"You ready to call it quits for the day?" she asked him.

"If you're tired, sure," he replied.

"I just don't want you to overdo it, that's all," Grace shot back.

"Me?" Dylan laughed. "I could keep digging all night." He stretched out his arms and winced at how stiff they were.

"Ha. Yeah, I see that." Grace grinned.

Just then Mr. Garcia came rolling up the main road in his six-wheel pickup truck, towing a trailer bed behind him. He waved at them just as he hit a bump. The trailer lifted off the ground, then slammed back down with a startling clatter—and Dylan knew what was about to happen. He spun around toward Brave just as the dog's head shot up on the other side of the field. Brave let out a terrified howl, then a frenzied, desperate barking that sounded like his very life was at stake. As the truck drove past, Brave hunched over, lowered his tail between his legs, and whined. He looked around frantically, ready to bolt.

"Brave, come!" Dylan called out before Brave could take off. Brave looked like he wanted to run as far from them as he could, but he didn't. Instead, he did as Dylan commanded and ran to his side. "Good boy," Dylan said, dropping to his knees and wrapping his arms around the dog, who shook like a leaf. "It's okay. Shhh . . . it's okay. It was just the truck, that's all, buddy."

Brave leaned into Dylan, breathing heavily.

"It's like every time he takes one step forward, he takes two steps back," Dylan said grimly.

"But at least he's taking the step forward," Grace said. "So we know it's possible for him to get past this. We just have to keep working with him."

"That would be great," Dylan said, feeling like a heavy cloud had descended over him, "except we're running out of time."

"Hey." Grace's voice was firm. "That's not how we talk on the Garcia Ranch."

"But we are. We only have three days—"

"That's right. We have three full days. Look how far he's come in just a week and a half, Dylan. Brave is so obedient now, and he trusts you. Your bond is amazing."

That much was true—Dylan couldn't deny it. It was almost as if the more Brave trusted him, the calmer and steadier the dog got.

"That's what's going to help him," Grace continued, sitting down on the ground next to Dylan and reaching out to scratch Brave behind his silky ears. "We can do this—*he* can do this. Your mom is going to see how great Brave is."

Mustang trotted over and lay down by Brave, as if she knew that being there would help her pal. With his arm around his dog, whose heart rate was coming down slowly,

Dylan looked out over the grassy field that they had worked so hard to clear. He felt the sun on his face and heard the gentle burbling of the creek nearby.

Dylan had grown up just down the road from where they sat, but the ranch might as well have been another planet — a planet he had never known he would love so much. Working there made him feel like he could do anything, and he had never felt so at home. For that moment, he wanted nothing more than to believe that Grace was right. That maybe the ranch would change Brave's life too, and they could do this.

Maybe they really could stay together.

★ CHAPTER 17 ★

Dylan stared at himself in the mirror. His stomach felt squirmy and his palms were clammy.

He couldn't do it.

He took the cowboy hat off and held it in his hands. Then he put it back on.

Part of Dylan's mind was always on the ranch. The clatter of machinery and the smells of the fields—and the barns—played on repeat in his head as he lay in bed at night or took notes in Social Studies. He closed his eyes and heard Mr. Garcia calling him and Grace inside at the end of the day. Without speaking, he and Grace would finish whatever they were doing and head toward the house to get cleaned up.

They had become a real team, too. But during the day at school, as if by silent agreement, Dylan and Grace acted like they barely knew each other. She still sat with her friends at lunch, and he sat with Jaxon and the guys. If they passed each other in the hall, they exchanged a quick hello and kept walking. It was almost as if Dylan spent his days on one world and his afternoons on another. And when he was on his own, he was trapped between the two, not sure which direction to go in.

But that morning, Dylan had woken up with a question heavy on his mind. Why did his two worlds have to be separate? Why couldn't he bring them together?

Which is how he found himself standing in front of the mirror, just minutes before he had to leave, spinning a cowboy hat in his hands and debating whether or not to wear it to school.

Why couldn't he wear it, like Grace and her friends wore theirs? Of course he'd be polite like they were and take it off during class or when he ate. But the rest of the time, he'd wear it with pride. He put the hat back on his head. It was Grace's brother's old one, and it fit him perfectly — just snug enough to stay put when he was riding Rey or bending over in the field. Dylan examined himself in the mirror, tapping on the brim and tipping the front of the hat down, the way real cowboys wore it.

Brave watched him from the bed.

"What do you think, buddy?" he asked Brave. "Can I

pull this off?" Brave yipped approvingly. Dylan looked at himself again in the mirror, turning from side to side and watching his hat turn with him. "Or am I just asking for trouble?" he said under his breath.

He sat down on the bed next to Brave, who wore his bandanna, and pulled out his phone to snap a selfie. He captioned it #cowboyduds before sending it to his dad.

Dylan closed his eyes and steeled himself. The hat was big, and once he left the house, he was stuck with it. It wasn't like he could throw it in a backpack. But why would he want to hide it? He'd earned the right to wear the hat—shouldn't he feel proud of his self-discipline and hard work? He took a deep breath. There was no more time to debate it. With a whistle at Brave, who hopped off the bed and followed him, Dylan headed out the door to school, the brown leather hat planted firmly on his head.

★ ★ ★

Dylan tried to ignore the surprised looks. Some of the kids in the hallway at school nodded approvingly, but others laughed and turned to whisper to their friends. Dylan's cheeks were burning, but he took a breath and exhaled slowly. *You got this*, he told himself.

Then he stepped through the doorway into English class. He quickly scanned the room, but Grace wasn't there yet. Jaxon, however, was.

Jaxon's eyes went wide, and a huge grin crossed his face. "Look who just walked in. Dude Ranch Dylan."

The other kids laughed nervously. Normally Dylan would have laughed too—and he definitely wouldn't have tried to stop Jaxon. But this time he was on the receiving end of his best friend's teasing, which sounded almost innocent but was just biting enough to sting. It made Dylan want to pull off the cowboy hat and run out of class. Another part of him knew that running away wasn't the answer, though. That wasn't what Grace would do. It wasn't what any of the cowboys on the ranch would do.

He was tired of hiding this side of himself at school. He loved the ranch and ranch life—and he shouldn't be afraid to show it.

Dylan sat down in his regular seat next to Jaxon, who let out a loud guffaw.

"Seriously, dude, what's on your head?" Jaxon said, loudly enough for the whole class to hear. "Halloween isn't for a few weeks." The kids around them snickered.

Dylan took a deep breath and told the truth.

"It's my hat. I wear it when I'm working."

"Working?" Jaxon chuckled.

"Yep. I've been working on the Garcia Ranch with Grace and my dog."

"A ranch? With Grace Garcia and that dog—what's his name, Brave? Wait, I thought you were grounded."

Something about Jaxon's tone was really getting under Dylan's skin. He didn't like the sound of Grace's and Brave's names in his mouth.

"I kind of lied about that," Dylan admitted. "But I'm done lying now."

"That's why you've been bailing on me?"

"Yeah."

Something flickered across Jaxon's face, and for a second Dylan thought he was hurt that Dylan had lied to him. But then Jaxon's expression hardened into something else.

"What do you do at the ranch, shovel up after the cows go number two?" Jaxon's tone was outright sneering now.

His words were like a slap, and it took Dylan a second to recover. "It's called mucking stables," Dylan replied. "And yeah, I've done it."

Jaxon looked at the kids sitting nearby. "D'you hear that? Dylan shovels poo!"

The kids laughed. Dylan felt his face go red. Maybe this had all been a terrible idea.

Jaxon scowled at him. "Good choice, dude," he said, his voice heavy with sarcasm. "That hat is obviously way cooler than making viral videos with me. It's funny that we used to be friends."

Dylan's whole body felt like it was on fire, and he was shaking. He stood up fast, clenching and unclenching his fists, trying not to let his hurt and anger show. Jaxon stood up too. "So you're saying we're not friends anymore?" Dylan asked.

"That depends," Jaxon said, locking his eyes on Dylan's. "Are you going to take off that hat and dress like a normal person?"

Dylan felt everyone else in the classroom staring at them as they stood facing each other. Jaxon held his gaze until Dylan broke it off, looking over Jaxon's shoulder. A poster tacked to the far wall said RESPECT ISN'T GIVEN, IT'S EARNED in all caps. Dylan looked down at the floor and scuffed his foot against the desk.

It was like there was a battle going on inside his brain. He knew that if he took off the hat, everything would go back to normal and Jaxon would stop making fun of him and their group of friends could go back to the way they used to be. But he loved the hat—and everything it stood for. Plus, Grace had given it to him as a gift.

"Last chance," Jaxon said.

Before Dylan could answer, Ms. Frantzis hustled into the room, looking frazzled.

"Let's get started, guys," she said, without looking up to see the standoff happening in her classroom.

Her presence broke the spell. Dylan gritted his teeth, reached up, and took the hat off. The cool air felt good on his head. He ran a hand through his hair and forced himself to smile. "It was just a joke," he said to Jaxon. "Why'd you have to take it so seriously?"

Jaxon cackled. "Seriously, dude? Nice one! You got me."

"You totally fell for it," Dylan said. He looked around at their classmates, who nodded in agreement and seemed relieved that the showdown had been a fake.

"Eyes up here," Ms. Frantzis called out with a clap of her hands. As everyone took their seats, Dylan put the hat on the floor under his chair. He twisted around to reach his backpack, and that's when he saw that Grace had come in and was sitting right behind him.

She had heard—and seen—the whole thing.

The look of sadness and betrayal on her face was more than Dylan could bear. He couldn't meet her eye, so instead he turned around to face forward again. There was a rustling sound, the *zzzzzt* of a zipper being hastily closed, footsteps, and then the click of the door shutting firmly.

Dylan spun back around. Grace's seat was empty. He looked to the doorway, but she was long gone.

He raised a hand into the air. "Sorry, Ms. Frantzis, but I

have to — I need to — I'll be right back." Dylan didn't wait for a response. He jumped out of his seat and ran into the hall, but it was empty.

Dylan's heart was beating a mile a minute. Should he go after her? Would she even speak to him? He hated that she'd witnessed any of what had just happened between him and Jaxon. But now she was gone, and he had no chance to explain it to her.

Just then, Jaxon stepped into the hall behind him and wrapped an arm around Dylan's shoulder. "Let her go," he stage-whispered. "And meet me after school. There's something I want to show you."

★ CHAPTER 18 ★

Apparently, Jaxon's plan involved biking three miles into the desert. They'd picked up Brave after school and were now forging their way off-trail. Dust swelled up around their bike tracks and the ground looked parched. It felt like the land was ripe for rain.

Dylan thought they had to be close to the reservoir, but at Jaxon's direction, they kept going—Jaxon leading and Brave running at Dylan's side—until they reached an open, hilly stretch of land. The day was hot and humid, and sweat dripped off the tip of Dylan's nose as they finally came to a stop in the middle of nowhere, way out of sight of any houses. Brave was panting too, and Dylan let him have a few gulps from his water bottle.

"This is the spot," Jaxon said as he shrugged off his backpack and it spilled open, revealing the contents inside.

"Uh, the spot for what?" Dylan couldn't believe his eyes. "What's all that?"

Jaxon clapped his hands together gleefully. "That, my friend, is a whole backpack full of fireworks."

Brave stepped over and sniffed at the bag, which sat on the ground between the boys.

"Brave, leave it," Dylan said. The nearly two weeks of training clicked in and Brave did as he was told. Turning his attention elsewhere, the dog sniffed his way around the desert clearing and the low, scruffy bushes. They were surrounded by layers of hills, a signature of the land northwest of San Antonio. There were a few spindly-looking trees and cacti scattered around too.

Dylan had never been this far away from home before on his own. He checked his phone. Service was spotty. His mom thought he was working on the ranch that afternoon, and he hoped she wouldn't try calling him—and get mad if it went straight to voicemail. Then he reminded himself that she'd be even angrier if she found out that he and Jaxon were about to set off fireworks.

"So, where'd you get them?" Dylan asked, nudging the bag with his toe. It was heavy and didn't budge an inch.

"You remember how I asked my dad for fireworks and he refused to buy them?"

"Yeah?"

"Well, I found my own connection. There's a kid who knows a kid who knows another kid. Seems like they had some left over from the Fourth of July."

"What does that mean?"

"Dude. It means I have fireworks. Stop asking questions and let's set them off. You said you'd be my wingman for a little adventure."

Dylan wasn't sure how to reply. His parents had always been firm about not letting him play with fireworks. He could practically hear the main points of their lecture replaying in his head: *Fireworks are dangerous, I knew a kid growing up who got hurt really badly, it's extra risky if you don't know who you're buying them from or how old they are* . . .

For about the hundredth time that afternoon, Dylan questioned whether he'd made the right choice by following Jaxon out into the desert. If he'd known Jaxon's plan was to set off fireworks, he'd have said no, and then he and Brave could have been hanging out with Grace, Mustang, and Rey on the ranch at that very moment.

Then, with a sharp pang, Dylan remembered that wasn't an option anymore. Because Dylan had messed up everything, turning around and high-tailing it to the comfort of the ranch was out of the question. He replayed the scene, seeing the wounded look on Grace's face and hearing the sound of the classroom door closing behind her as she took off. He remembered that he had made his choice: Jaxon.

Dylan was miserable. He knew he'd been cruel to his new friend, who had never been anything but kind to him. And because of it he wouldn't be welcome on the Garcia Ranch anymore—not today, not ever.

"Check this out—" Jaxon was waving a small paper-wrapped tube with a wick in front of Dylan's face.

Dylan swatted it away. "Jax—not in my face, man."

Jaxon laughed. "It's not lit, dummy."

"How are you going to do it?" Dylan asked, changing the subject.

Jaxon held out a plastic grocery bag that had been dangling from his handlebars the whole way. Dylan took it and peered inside. It was a watermelon.

"We're going to stuff this thing with fireworks and blow it up," Jaxon said. "Film the whole thing, in slo-mo on my phone and regular speed on yours, then edit them together and put it on YouTube. Exploding fruit videos! We're totally going viral."

"Um . . . isn't it kind of dangerous to light that many fireworks at once?"

"I thought you were up for this," Jax said, his eyebrows raised.

"I mean, of course I am," Dylan stammered.

"Watermelon meets fireworks." Jaxon laughed. "That's all kinds of awesome."

Dylan nodded nervously. He eyed the underbrush and wondered just how dry—and flammable—it was. Brave was thoroughly investigating the area with his nose, nudging at rocks and pawing at piles of twigs. A small rodent of some kind panicked at the sight of him and scurried off with a terrified squeak. Brave barked and started after it.

"Brave—stop!" Dylan commanded him. Disappointed, Brave stopped and trotted back toward him. "Good boy," Dylan said, giving the dog a treat from his pocket.

"Dude, your dog is nuts," Jaxon said with a shake of his head.

Dylan bristled. Brave had literally just demonstrated how well trained he was by obeying a command, but all Jaxon could see was that he was a bad dog. *Whatever*, Dylan told himself.

He wished he knew how to get out of this situation—not just for himself, but for Brave, too. The sound of a ton of fireworks going off at once was going to be loud and scary. Dylan knew Brave was definitely going to be freaked out by it, but just how bad would his reaction be? And how could he get himself and the dog out of this without having to hear a ton of grief from Jaxon? He already thought Brave was a nuisance—what would he say if Dylan told him he couldn't stay because Brave would be scared of the fireworks?

It would never work, and he'd never live it down at school. And now that he'd hurt Grace's feelings so badly, Jaxon and the other guys were the only friends Dylan had.

Dylan was stuck. And so was Brave.

While Jaxon cut a hole in the side of the watermelon with a pocket knife and started scooping out some of the flesh, Dylan scanned the area and spotted a tree a few yards away. It was the sturdiest-looking of the bunch. He led Brave over to it and wrapped his leash around the lowest branch, then clipped it to Brave's collar. Brave whimpered as Dylan started to walk away.

"I know, pal," Dylan said to the dog. "It's just for a minute though, okay? I'll be right back for you and then we can go home." At least this way Brave wouldn't be able to go anywhere. And maybe, just maybe, Brave had overcome his fears enough—and it would all be over quickly enough —that the dog would be okay.

Jaxon had packed the watermelon with fireworks so that their wicks dangled out of it. He wiped his sticky hands on his shorts, then took out a lighter and his phone. Dylan stood a few feet away, close to Brave.

"Get closer, dude!" Jaxon said. "You'll never get a good shot from way back there. You got your camera ready?"

Dylan took a couple of steps forward and took his phone out of his pocket. He set the camera to record video and nodded that he was ready. His heart drummed hard in his chest. Brave whined from his spot by the tree, like he knew something was about to happen.

Jaxon held up his phone and flicked the lighter. He held the flame under the first wick, which quickly caught and sparked all the others. A loud hiss filled the air as the strings blackened and curled up toward their roots.

Dylan held his breath. The air went still. And then . . . *BOOM!*

It was the loudest noise he had ever heard. It started with one large blast that vibrated his chest, then was followed by a dozen or more smaller pops and bursts from within the large cloud of gray smoke that encircled them.

Through the noise, Dylan heard something else—a sound that was at once familiar and upsetting. It was Brave, and he was terrified. The dog was crying out, wailing and howling and yelping so loudly that it was painful to hear. Dylan spun around just in time to see Brave pulling with all his strength on the leash that lashed him to the tree branch.

"Brave, no—" Dylan shouted, but it was too late. With a loud crack, the branch snapped off and the dog was free. With one final wail—and without a backward glance— Brave sped off and was out of sight within seconds.

Dylan's phone slipped from his fingers and landed in the dirt as he raced after the dog, fear coursing through his veins and his ears still echoing from the explosion.

★ CHAPTER 19 ★

"Brave!" Dylan was hoarse from screaming the dog's name over and over. His voice echoed off the rocks and bounced back at him, but Brave still didn't appear. "Brave—come back!"

Either Brave had forgotten all of his training in an instant, or he had traveled so far, so fast that he was already out of earshot. Neither was a good option.

Dylan had raced away from their bikes and the spot of the blown up watermelon, but he could still hear Jaxon calling him. He didn't want to stop searching for Brave, but the terrain was unfamiliar and he had no water or supplies with him. With one last scan of the horizon, he turned and headed back. Crestfallen, he trudged across the dry landscape toward Jaxon, who was hunched over something on the ground.

Just as Dylan got close, he smelled burning and saw

Jaxon jump backward. There, on the ground, a stack of fire-crackers smoldered until, with a deafening burst, they went off one after the other. *Bam! Bam! Bam!*

Jaxon let out a gleeful hoot and punched the air.

"What are you doing?" Dylan shouted. "Brave will never come back if you keep making all that noise!"

Jaxon looked at Dylan as if he'd grown a second head. "Chill, seriously. We had some extras." He shook his head. "It's like aliens took over my best friend or something. What happened? You used to be fun."

"My dog just ran away," Dylan said, astonished at the way Jaxon was acting.

"He was a stray, right?"

Dylan nodded.

"So he ran away." Jaxon waved a hand in the general direction Brave had fled. "That's what strays do, isn't it? Did you get the shot, by the way?"

Dylan was confused. "The shot? What shot—"

"The video!" Jaxon laughed. "The whole reason we're out here, Dylan."

Dylan blinked, trying to process his friend's words, but he could barely take in what Jaxon was saying. All he cared about right now was finding Brave. He dug his phone out of the dirt and handed it over to Jaxon. "I don't care if I got 'the shot.' I have to find Brave. And since you dragged me all the way out here, you better be coming with."

"Seriously? He'll come back, Dyl."

"He won't. Not unless we go find him." He studied his friend's familiar face, looking for any sign of the kid he'd grown up with. "Please—can you just help me, Jaxon?"

Jaxon gave him a grudging shrug. "Fine." He took a few steps toward the brush and halfheartedly called Brave's name.

They circled the area for half an hour, and Dylan was grateful to see that Jaxon was actually trying to help. He peered behind rocks and under shrubs and squinted at gray shadows in the distance—but no luck. Either Brave couldn't hear them or he didn't want to be found. With every passing minute, Dylan grew more worried that his dog was long gone, swallowed up by the Texas wilderness.

"Seriously, Dyl, we're never going to find him." Jaxon spoke Dylan's worst fear out loud. "I don't know what to tell you."

Dylan had never felt worse. Brave was gone, and there was no way to track him. Unless . . . Dylan buried his face in his hands. There *was* one person who might be able to find Brave. But it would take one huge apology, and even that might not be enough.

"I have an idea," Dylan said to Jaxon. "It's not a very good one, but it's better than nothing."

Jaxon looked annoyed, but he bit his lip. "What is it?"

"I think Grace can help us."

"For real?" Jaxon looked skeptical. "Her? How exactly can she help you that I can't?"

"She's actually pretty cool," Dylan said. "And she's amazing with animals—Brave really trusts her. Plus . . ." He took a deep breath and exhaled slowly. "She's my friend, Jaxon."

With just a slight shake of his head, Jaxon hopped onto his bike. "Lead the way."

★ ★ ★

It was late afternoon by the time Dylan skidded through the iron gate of the Garcia Ranch. He steered around a tractor moving at a snail's pace down the main road. The ranch hand in the driver's seat waved at Dylan as he passed, but Dylan was too focused on reaching Grace to notice.

He found her in the corral, running Rey through a warmup.

"Grace!" Dylan called.

He couldn't tell if she heard him or not, but she rode in the opposite direction and over to the far end of the ring without even looking at Dylan.

Dylan hopped off his bike and ran to the fence. He put one foot on the bottom rail and stood up on it. "Grace!"

he shouted again. This time she couldn't ignore him. She walked Rey back slowly and pulled in the reins, stopping a few feet from Dylan. Jaxon rode up behind Dylan, and Grace narrowed her eyes in his direction.

"Is this some kind of joke?" she asked coolly. She trained her eyes on the horizon over their heads.

"No—" Dylan's voice cracked and he stopped to take a breath. "Grace, I'm really sorry about today at school—about the hat."

She didn't speak but waited for him to continue.

"It's Brave," Dylan said. "He's gone."

Grace's eyes snapped to Dylan's. "What do you mean, 'gone'?"

"I mean we were out in the hills—" Dylan jerked a thumb toward Jaxon. "And we—he—there were fireworks—"

"Fireworks?" she interrupted him.

"Yes." Dylan was ashamed to admit it, but he couldn't lie to Grace. She shook her head in disbelief. "And Brave got spooked and took off," he went on. "I looked for him for so long but I couldn't find him and he wouldn't come back . . ." Dylan trailed off. "I thought he would be okay."

"You pushed him too far," Grace said, her voice stern. "Fireworks are too much for him—they're like a hundred times worse than other noises!"

Dylan hung his head. "I know. It's all my fault. But I

really need your help, Grace—please. I need help finding him."

"Dylan, we worked so hard all this time—Brave worked so hard. How could you do this?"

He didn't answer. There was nothing to say.

"So, uh, can you help us or not, Grace?" Jaxon called out from behind Dylan. "'Cause if not, I'm going to head home."

So much for being helpful, Dylan thought as he shot a look at his friend. The more Jaxon acted like that, the less likely Grace was going to help them.

"Sorry." Jaxon held up his hands and shook his head. "Just saying."

Grace glared at Jaxon, then turned her steely gaze on Dylan. "Fine."

Dylan held his breath. "Fine?"

"I'll help you," she said with a frustrated sigh. She hopped down off Rey and led him by the reins toward the barn. "But I'm doing this for Brave. Not for you."

"Thank you—I'll make it up to you," Dylan said. "Whatever it takes. I just—I just want everything to be okay again." Struggling to balance his old friend, his new friend, and the dog he had come to love, Dylan had never meant anything more in his life.

★ CHAPTER 20 ★

Dylan filled three water bottles and stuffed them into the backpack. Grace tossed him a bag of beef jerky, six granola bars, and a plastic baggie of kibble, which he dropped in too.

Jaxon stood awkwardly by the front door, looking around Grace's home like he wasn't quite sure how he had ended up there.

Mustang sniffed around Dylan's feet, then made her way over to Grace. She whimpered and pawed at Grace's leg.

"You're staying here," Grace said. "Sorry, girl. But I have no idea where we're going to end up, and I don't want you out there—especially if it gets dark." She checked the time on her phone, then looked out the window and up at the sky. "We need to get going," she said.

"I'm ready," Dylan said, zipping up the pack and swinging it onto his shoulder.

"Me too," Grace said. She and Dylan looked over at Jaxon.

"Ready," he said, raising an eyebrow. Dylan couldn't read Jaxon's tone—was he being sarcastic? He didn't seem like he really wanted to help, but if he didn't, then why was he still there? Why was he coming with them? There was no time to figure it out, though—they had to go.

Dylan and Jaxon got on their bikes, and Dylan was surprised to see Grace rolling hers out of the garage.

"You're taking your bike?" he asked her.

She rolled her eyes at him. "What—you think the Ranch Kids can only ride horses or something?"

Dylan gulped. So she *did* know what he and Jaxon and the others called them. "No . . . sorry . . . I didn't mean—" he stammered.

"Trust me, I'd be much faster on Rey than on a bike." Grace shot Dylan a pointed look. "But if Brave is really freaked out, then he's taken a big step back in his training and the horse might scare him off. And that's exactly what we don't want."

"Right."

It occurred to Dylan then that there was something so different about Grace. She wasn't like other kids their age —she saw things much more clearly. It was almost as if she was always thinking two or three steps ahead, while he was barely keeping up with whatever was happening right then.

He was so grateful she had agreed to come find Brave, even if he didn't completely deserve her help.

★ ★ ★

They rode quickly through the afternoon sunlight, returning to the spot in the hills where splatters of watermelon still stained the dirt. The three of them stood side by side, scanning the horizon for signs of Brave. The air was so humid it felt like they could touch it.

"Have you been here before?" Grace asked Jaxon.

"All the time," he said. He shot Dylan a sideways glance. "What?" Jaxon asked defensively. "Sure, I come here to do stuff sometimes."

"Like blow up watermelons with fireworks?" Dylan asked.

"Yeah, so what?"

"So what?" Dylan's jaw dropped open. "It's dangerous, that's what."

"Guys—" Grace held up a hand. "Can you work that out later?"

"Sorry," Dylan said.

"Anyway, as I was saying," Grace said to Jaxon. "You know this area pretty well?"

Dylan thought he knew where Grace was going with this. "Is there any place you can think of where Brave might hide?"

Jaxon pointed toward a cluster of boulders about a half-mile off to the right. "That's a great hiding spot. Lots of room under the rocks. Even a cave or two."

Dylan turned to Jaxon. "Why didn't you tell me that before? We could have searched there earlier!"

"I don't know—you didn't ask, I guess," Jaxon shot back. "Dylan, why are you acting like this is all my fault? I didn't bring the dog out here in the first place—you did!"

"No, but you—"

"*Guys!*" Grace shouted. "Enough."

Dylan clenched his jaw. "Fine. Whatever. Let's go."

Dylan took the lead as they biked across the rough terrain, following a bumpy trail that got rockier the farther they went. When they reached the pyramid of rocks, stacked twice as tall as Dylan and as wide as an eighteen-wheeler, they threw their bikes to the ground and clambered up the side. They peered around, behind, and between the boulders.

"Brave!" Dylan called.

"Brave . . . here, boy!" Grace shouted. "Brave!"

There was no sign of the dog. Dylan kicked the dirt in frustration, sending a spray of pebbles flying.

"Let's keep going," Grace said. She looked up at the sky uncertainly. A thick layer of clouds had slid into place above them and begun to block the sun.

"Can we hurry?" Jaxon said. "My parents are going to start wondering where I am soon."

Dylan ignored him. He knew his mom would be wondering the same thing, but he was too focused on finding Brave to worry about it. He hoped she'd understand—and promised himself he'd text her as soon as they got back into range of service.

They pushed along. The ground got bumpier, strewn with more and bigger rocks, until the trail petered out completely. The vegetation around them thickened and pressed in on them as they headed down a slope toward a dry creek bed. They were covered in dust, which turned to muddy sweat in the humidity, and cactus prickles stuck to their pants.

It was getting harder to ride their bikes without a clear path. Dylan swerved to avoid a rock as big as a toaster and slammed his front tire into a slightly smaller one. He ditched the bike just in time to avoid flying over the handlebars, but his bike landed with a hard thud.

"I think we have to leave our bikes here, guys," Grace said, pulling to a short stop behind him. "There's no more trail this far out."

Dylan couldn't argue with her, but it was hard going. "Okay," he said. "Let's keep moving on foot."

They propped their bikes against a huge flat rock in the

center of the creek bed. At least they'd have a good land-mark on the way back home.

They trekked on for what felt like miles. Every few steps, Dylan stopped shouting Brave's name and listened carefully for the faintest sound of a whimper or a bark. But there was nothing — not even the rustling of leaves or the scuttling of a rodent. Just as Dylan realized that it was weirdly still and quiet, like it usually was right before a storm, he felt the first drop of rain land on his arm.

"Oh, dude —" Jaxon groaned. "Seriously?"

Dylan couldn't have agreed more, but he knew his reasons were different from Jaxon's. Jaxon just didn't want to get wet, but Dylan didn't care about that. He didn't mind getting soaked if it would help him find his dog — but he was worried that the weather would only make it harder for them to find Brave. If the dog was hiding, he might not want to come out in the rain, or he might not hear them over the sound of it.

He just hoped there wasn't thunder.

Dylan turned his face to the darkening sky right as it opened up and the humidity broke, dropping a deluge of raindrops that pelted him on the face and arms, hard. His skin stung, and within seconds all three of them were fully soaked. It was a true Texas rainstorm, which meant it was possible it could be over in a few minutes — or go on for hours. With their luck, Dylan figured it might continue all evening. He hoped Brave had managed to find shelter, at least.

Dylan looked over at Grace, who held a hand above her eyes to shield them from the water. They caught each other's gaze, and as they did, a crack of lightning lit up the sky. Then, a few seconds later, the air began to rumble and shake all around them, the sound rising and rolling until it transformed into an angry clap of thunder. It was so loud they both jumped, and Dylan felt his eardrums vibrating.

Dylan and Grace didn't need to speak to know what the other one was thinking.

Thunder was bad. The sound of it would terrify Brave. And the more scared he was, the harder it would be to find him.

"This is bad," Dylan said, nearly shouting to be heard over the rain.

"It's not good," Grace replied.

Another flash of lightning lit up the sky so brightly that it burned his eyes, and he squeezed them shut. Seconds passed with just the sound of the pounding rain, and then a crash of thunder shook the sky again.

Dylan pointed back toward the rocks they had just searched. Grace nodded and gestured at Jaxon to follow them. The three of them dashed across the soaked land. The water was coming down too fast for the ground to absorb it, and puddles had sprung up everywhere. They reached the rock formation and huddled in a small alcove formed by two leaning boulders, which didn't entirely block the rain but offered some cover.

Dylan could feel the water dripping inside his clothes. He tried to wipe his face on his sleeve but only succeeded in smearing water around. Dylan shook his head and squeezed his eyes shut—all he wanted to do was find Brave, but instead it felt like he was losing him even more. "This is the worst!" he exclaimed, punching his fist into his palm.

"I'm sorry, Dylan," Grace said. "I know this is tough, but we're going to find Brave."

"Wrong," Jaxon said. Dylan's and Grace's heads both shot toward him, their mouths agape. "You know what this is?" Jaxon went on, his face screwed up into a scowl. "It's pointless. I mean, we're never going to find your dog. It's gone. There's absolutely no point in us staying out here in the rain, dude—let's just get out of here."

Anger and frustration rose up in Dylan like a tidal wave. He had thought Jaxon was on his side, but he was wrong. Jaxon wasn't on anyone's side but his own. Dylan had tried to be patient with him. Time after time, he'd tried to do what his friend wanted to do—even when it was the last thing

Dylan wanted. He'd tried to be what his friend wanted him to be. But he couldn't fake it anymore. Dylan clenched his fists and took a deep breath, waiting until his anger subsided enough for him to speak without yelling.

Dylan opened his mouth, but no words came out at first. Then he found his voice.

"You know what, Jaxon?" Dylan said. "You're being so mean."

"Excuse me?" Jaxon's eyebrows shot straight up his forehead.

"First of all," Dylan went on, "Brave is a *he,* not an *it.* And second of all, you could at least pretend to care that my dog is gone. That's what a real friend would do."

"I am your *real* friend," Jaxon sputtered. "Why else would I be out here?"

"I don't know," Dylan said. "Why *are* you really here?"

Grace looked from one boy to the other, holding her breath.

Jaxon held up both hands. "To help you."

"I don't believe you," Dylan said. "Tell me the truth."

Jaxon looked at the ground, then the rain, then the rocks over Dylan's shoulder. Dylan let him squirm and waited for him to speak.

"Fine," Jaxon said. "I'm here because you need help.

Aaaand . . ." He paused. "If I help you, maybe you won't tell my parents about the fireworks. That's all. A little trade, basically."

Dylan shook his head in disbelief. "I knew it."

"It's just a dog," Jaxon said dismissively. "He'll turn up."

"But he's *my* dog. Doesn't that mean anything?" Dylan couldn't believe this was his oldest friend—the one who had been there in the outfield next to him at their first Little League game. Who had eaten lunch with him every day for all of elementary school. And who had wandered the halls with him on the first day of middle school, looking as nervous and overwhelmed by the huge building as Dylan was. But that was Jaxon then. This was who Jaxon was now.

"It means that I don't get it, Dyl," Jaxon said. "I don't get why this is such a big deal. The dog is a stray—it'll find its way back."

"*Brave*," Dylan said. "His name is Brave. And honestly, he's a way better friend than you are."

"Look," Jaxon said. "I get that you're upset about the d—*Brave*. And I'm sorry he's gone. But can you not be mad at me because he ran away? It's not my fault."

As angry as he was, Dylan knew Jaxon was right. It wasn't Jaxon's fault that Brave was spooked by loud noises, and it wasn't even his fault that he'd been the one to light the fireworks. Dylan didn't have to come out to the hills with Jaxon. Dylan didn't have to bring Brave. And Dylan didn't have to tie the dog to a tree instead of holding him securely.

But Dylan was out here trying to help Brave—and fix all of his own mistakes. Jaxon was out here so that Dylan wouldn't get him in trouble. Not because he actually cared.

And for Dylan, that wasn't enough. If Jaxon wasn't there to help him for real, then Dylan didn't want him there at all. He'd had it with the way Jaxon had been acting for days . . . weeks . . . months, even. He had turned into a person that Dylan barely recognized, and just because the other guys let him get away with it didn't mean Dylan had to. Plus, he realized in that moment, no one else would ever have the guts to stand up to Jaxon—it had to be him. Otherwise Jaxon would never stop being this way.

Dylan was done.

"You used to be a good guy, Jaxon," Dylan said, keeping his voice steady. "But now you're just not. And you're a bad friend."

Jaxon's jaw fell open. He stared at Dylan for a long moment, as if he was wasn't sure what he'd really heard. Then he snapped his mouth shut, narrowed his eyes, and scrambled out from under the rocks. He slipped in the mud, but caught himself.

"I'm going home," Jaxon said.

Without a glance back at Dylan, he stomped off through the driving rain.

★ CHAPTER 21 ★

Dylan swallowed hard and looked down at the ground. He felt a sharp pain in his hands and realized he'd been clenching his fists and digging his fingernails into his palms. He stretched out his fingers. Grace seemed to sense that he needed a second and didn't speak right away.

"You okay?" she finally asked.

Dylan nodded, though he wasn't actually sure if he was. Mostly he was confused—he knew he'd only told Jaxon the truth, and that Jaxon needed to hear it. But then why did Dylan feel so terrible for saying those things? Shouldn't he be feeling better, not worse? At the moment, all he felt was queasy.

"You know you did the right thing, right?" Grace said, raising an eyebrow. It was as if she could read his mind.

Dylan's head shot up. "I did?"

"Yeah. Telling him off like that took guts."

"I guess," Dylan said. "But it didn't do any good. He just took off anyway." Dylan felt a twinge of guilt—he hadn't wanted Jaxon there anymore—but also sadness as the reality sank in. The fact that Jaxon would split like that only confirmed what Dylan already knew: Their friendship was a one-way street that didn't run in Dylan's direction. If it wasn't good for Jaxon, Jaxon wasn't interested in it. That was no way to be a friend. *But it still sucks,* Dylan thought. "He wasn't always like this."

"I know. I remember him in elementary school. He wasn't so bad."

"I'm not sure what changed," Dylan said. "But I wish it would change back." He buried his face in his hands and groaned. "I can't believe I just said all that to him. He'll never speak to me again."

"He will." Grace placed a hand on his shoulder reassuringly. "I don't know why, but sometimes it's hardest to stand up to the people who deserve it the most."

Dylan nodded in agreement.

"And Jaxon definitely deserved it," Grace added.

"He really did," Dylan said.

"I'm not trying to tell you not to be friends with him," Grace said. "I just think you deserve better, that's all."

Dylan snuck a sideways glance at Grace. Her long black

hair was plastered to her face, and her wet clothes were suctioned to her skin. She had to be totally uncomfortable, but she was still there, still helping him find Brave. They hadn't even been friends that long, but something about Grace was true and loyal . . . the way Jaxon had once been.

"Thanks," Dylan said.

"For what?"

"For sticking this out with me."

"You're welcome." Grace pressed her lips together and nodded. "Just so we're clear, though—you know I'm still mad at you, right?"

Dylan laughed. "I know. And I deserve it."

"Yup. You do."

He looked out at the rain, which had started to slow down a little. The whole reason they were there came back to him like a punch in the gut. "How are we going to find Brave?" he asked.

Grace sighed. "By getting soaked."

"You mean more soaked?" Dylan asked.

"Can you get more soaked? Or is there only one level of soakedness?" she asked.

"I guess we're about to find out. Come on." Dylan squeezed out from under the rocks and let the rain pour down on him. He ignored the squish of water in his sneakers and the clammy feeling of his pants clinging to his legs. They sloshed through the muddy puddles, the water up to their ankles, back in the direction they'd been heading.

They made their way up a steep slope, but it got so slippery that they could barely stay upright. Dylan's right foot came down on top of a slick rock, and his ankle twisted underneath him. Grace's hand shot out to steady him, but she didn't catch him in time. He hit the ground hard, landing on his back with his head pointing downhill. He'd had the wind knocked out of him, and before he could catch his breath, he realized he was still moving . . . sliding this time, with sharp points scraping his skin and poking him in the ribs.

"Dylan!" Grace cried, moving as quickly—and carefully—as she could down the slope after him. "Are you okay?"

He slowed to a stop and lay still for a second while his heart rate recovered. "Oof—" He covered his face with his arms as a shower of small rocks ricocheted and whacked into him with a *ping ping ping*. "I'm fine," he said finally.

Grace reached his side. "I wasn't sure you were going to stop."

"Me neither."

Standing over him, she extended a hand. They gripped each other's wrists to get a firm hold, and she pulled him up to a standing position. He put all his weight on his good foot, gingerly holding the other one off the ground.

Grace sucked in her breath. "Ouch. Can you walk on it?"

"I think so." Dylan put his foot down and a jolt of searing pain shot up his leg. He winced from the pain and lifted it back up, still holding on to Grace for balance.

"Try again," she said. "Go slower this time."

Dylan took a breath and put the ball of his foot down first, then slowly lowered his heel. It still hurt, but less. He wriggled his toes to get the blood flowing again.

"Good," Grace said. "You're doing great. Easy."

"Yup." Exhaling slowly, he put more weight on his twisted ankle. "It's sore but I think it's okay."

She let go of his arm and he stood by himself. "You're very calm under pressure," she observed. "Not everyone's like that, you know."

"No?"

"No."

A crack of lightning and rumble of thunder reminded them that they needed to keep moving.

"You good?" Grace asked.

"I'm good. Walking it off. Let's go." Dylan stepped carefully up the slope and back onto flatter land. "Brave!" he cried, cupping his hands over his mouth. Still nothing.

They trekked and called, then trekked and called some more. All the while the rain pounded down and Dylan's ankle throbbed, but he barely noticed. He was too distracted by the question that weighed heavily on him—a question he hated saying out loud. But the more he turned it around in his mind, the less he could keep it to himself. "Do you think Brave's okay?"

"I don't know." Grace's face was tight with worry, and he could tell she'd been wondering the same thing. "This storm might really scare him. But he was on his own for a long time, and he knows how to take care of himself."

"We just need to find him—fast."

They kept up a steady pace. Dylan made a mental note of how far they'd come from the spot where Jaxon had blown up the watermelon and where they'd left their bikes. They'd need to be able to get back there once they found Brave. *If* they found Brave.

"Brave!" Grace called out.

"Here, boy!" Dylan shouted. "Come on, buddy—it's us!" His throat was getting raw, but he didn't stop. "Braaaaaave! Where are you?"

There was a faint murmur under the sound of the rain —so soft that Dylan wasn't sure he had really heard it.

Dylan froze. He looked at Grace—she had heard it too. He held a finger to his lips and strained his ears.

There it was. It was a bark. It was Brave.

★ CHAPTER 22 ★

They lost the sound of Brave's bark almost as soon as it started. Just as the rainfall surged and grew heavy again, the wind picked up, blocking out all other sound.

"Where is he?" Dylan shouted to Grace.

"I don't know," she replied. "Wait until the wind dies down again—we'll hear him."

"I hope so."

Dylan scanned the hilly landscape, which rose and fell in every direction. Flows of rainwater rushed around trees, cactuses, and underbrush, running off of smooth limestone plateaus and merging into muddy currents below. The heavy clouds had blocked out any remaining sunlight, and it was getting too dark to spot the dog.

There was nothing to do but wait. Every nerve in Dylan's body was on alert, and his senses were cranked up high. The wind paused, and in the silence that followed, he heard a quick bark, followed by whining, echoing off rock and dying out just as it reached them.

Dylan looked in the direction of the sound. "There!" He pointed at a tall, wide rock ledge at the bottom of a long slope, about a hundred yards away. Another bark floated on the air toward them.

"I hear him!" Grace responded, but Dylan had already taken off. He moved as fast as he could, but it was slow going over the sludgy, uneven ground. He felt like he was trapped in the bad dream he'd had many times—where he's trying to outrun a giant monster but he can barely get his heavy feet to move. Dylan slid and stumbled, tripping over downed tree branches and ignoring the pain in his ankle. Grace was right behind him.

They were halfway there. Dylan heard the bark again. "I'm coming, Brave!" he shouted. "Just hang on!"

"Oh no—" Grace cried out right behind him. Dylan spun around in time to see her lose her balance and start to fall forward. He threw out his arms to catch her just before she went down.

"I got you," he said.

"Thank you," Grace gasped. "That was close."

Just then, the air around them came alive, as if it had been electrified. Dylan felt pressure on his eardrums as the storm suddenly took on a new dimension. In an instant, the wind doubled in intensity, howling in his ears and knocking into him so hard he swayed on his feet. It swept across the land, tilting trees sideways and stripping off their leaves. The rain beat down even harder.

"Looks like the storm was just getting warmed up," Grace said. "We need to hurry."

As if in response, a bolt of lightning flashed, so bright it hurt their eyes. Thunder shook the air almost instantly, which meant the lightning had hit close by and the storm was right on top of them. The louder and more frequent the thunder, the more frightened Brave would be. And then he'd definitely take off again before they could find him!

This was going to be bad. Very, very bad.

They had to get to Brave.

A desperate bark rang out.

"Go!" Grace said to Dylan. "I'm right behind you."

Dylan ran toward Brave's cries faster than he'd ever run in his life.

He was three seconds away.

Two seconds away.

One second away . . . Dylan reached a cluster of rocks that rose high above his head just as Brave let out a desperate, terrified yowl that nearly broke his heart. The yelp sounded so close—he had to be within arm's reach. But where was he? Dylan couldn't see him anywhere. The dog's cries almost seemed to be coming from within the rock itself . . . but how? Dylan followed the sound, scrambling up onto a flat stone and peering down into a dark crevice behind it. In a flash of lightning that illuminated everything, he saw two frightened eyes staring back out at him.

Brave!

The dog stood up on his hind legs and scratched at the slick rock walls, but he couldn't pull himself out. He had to have fallen into the narrow space and gotten trapped.

Dylan jumped down next to Brave and reached for him just as thunder broke free from the sky. It boomed so loudly Dylan felt it in his whole body. He wanted to cover his ears, but he couldn't because he had grabbed hold of the shivering, soaking wet dog.

Dylan pulled Brave in close to his chest as the thunder rumbled around them. He curled himself over the dog to protect him from the sound, the vibration, the rain—everything. Brave sank into his arms, whimpering. Brave's breath was shallow and rapid, and Dylan could feel his heart pounding through his fur.

"I've got you, Brave," he whispered into the top of the dog's head. "It's okay—I'm here now. You're okay."

When the thunder finally stopped, Dylan pulled away and checked the dog over. Except for a few brambles in his fur and a serious wet dog smell, Brave seemed unharmed.

And now he was safe. Dylan squeezed his eyes shut. He was overcome with emotion, flooded by all the fear that they were never going to find Brave—or wouldn't find him until it was too late. But soon, as he held his dog tightly, Dylan's worry was washed away by relief. He buried his face in Brave's neck.

"I'm so glad you're okay, buddy," Dylan said. "And I'm sorry—I never should have brought you out here. I never should have tied you up or made you listen to those fireworks or go anywhere near Jaxon. It's all my fault—I'll never do that to you again, I promise. I'm so sorry I lost you."

"You can give yourself a bit more credit, you know."

Dylan looked up to see Grace standing on the flat rock above them, staring down at him with a funny look on her face.

"What do you mean?" Dylan asked her.

"I mean you didn't just lose him—you *found* him too. Give yourself a little credit."

Dylan thought about that for a second. Maybe Grace was right. After all they had been through in just a short time —after all the mistakes he'd made—he and Brave were together again. Wasn't that all that mattered in the end? It seemed like Brave had forgiven him, and Dylan swore to himself that he was never going to let his dog down again.

But Grace was wrong about one thing.

"Correction," Dylan said to her with a grin. "*We* found him."

Before Grace could answer, lightning lit up the dark sky behind her. "Look—" Grace pointed past Dylan to a shallow alcove tucked into the rock—"we can take cover there." She hopped down and they clambered into the opening just as the thunder bellowed again. The space was more like a wide overhang than a cave, and water dripped down its walls. But it kept them out of the direct rain, and they could all fit.

Dylan held the dog close. It was a relief to get out of the rain and wind, and they sat down on the hard ground and leaned back against the rock surface. Dylan closed his eyes and exhaled, catching his breath. Brave—who still had his leash attached—shifted in Dylan's arms, spinning around so he could lie down on his lap.

Brave's trembling began to subside as he settled down, though his ears were up and twitching, still hyperalert. Dylan flinched at one particularly loud crack of thunder, and Brave jumped in his arms, hopping to his feet and barking at the air.

"Easy, boy," Dylan said soothingly. "Shhhhh." He stroked Brave's ears and scratched the top of his head. As the dog slowly stopped shaking, Dylan understood that he had the power to soothe him, just as he had the ability to make him anxious. He needed to stay calm in order to keep Brave calm.

Brave sniffed at Dylan's cheek, snuffling and snorting, then licked the water off his face. Then he licked Dylan's ear. Then his nose. Then his forehead. Soon, Brave was up on all fours, his tail wagging a mile a minute as he let Dylan know how happy he was to see him.

"Look how much you're helping him," Grace said with a smile. At the sound of her voice, Brave turned his head in her direction and proceeded to lick her face from top to bottom, starting with her chin and making his way up to her forehead. "I love you too, Brave," she mumbled.

After Brave had run out of surface area to lick, he climbed back into Dylan's lap, spun around in a circle, and curled up into a tight little ball. Dylan was glad the dog wasn't freaking out anymore — he hated seeing him that upset. He held Brave close, and Grace huddled in for warmth. They stayed like that, quiet and comfortable and safe for the moment.

"Grace?" Dylan broke the silence.

"Yeah?"

"Brave has gotten so much better," Dylan said. "But do you think he can ever totally get over his trauma? Like, could he really be calm during a storm?"

Grace thought about it for a second. "He's made a lot of

progress," she said. "But I don't know if he'd be this relaxed if you weren't here. He trusts you." She paused. "He needs you."

The feeling, Dylan thought as he pressed his cheek against the top of Brave's head, was mutual.

After what felt like an hour, the rain and wind began to subside, and the thunder moved farther and farther into the distance. The cloud cover broke open overhead, and a single ray of late-afternoon sunshine burst through. Brave's head shot up at the sight of it, and his tail began to wag.

"Whewwwww." Dylan whistled.

"I think it's over," Grace said.

They stood up and brushed themselves off.

"Come on, Brave," Dylan said, reaching down to scratch the dog under the collar. "Let's go home."

★ CHAPTER 23 ★

Dylan didn't care that his toes were squishing around in his shoes. That his feet were squelching in mud and he was soaked to the bone—or that his ankle was still sore. He didn't even mind that they had trekked a lot farther than he realized, and it was a long way back to their bikes. He was just so glad to have Brave back that he would happily have traveled twice as far under worse circumstances.

Brave stuck to Dylan like glue. Dylan held on to his leash, but there was no need. Brave trotted right by his leg, and if Dylan slowed down, Brave slowed down. If Dylan stumbled, Brave stopped and nudged him with his snout to be sure he was all right.

"He's so happy to see you," Grace said. "I don't think he's ever leaving your side again."

Dylan reached down and scratched Brave under the collar. "Fine with me." Brave looked up at him lovingly, wagged his tail, and let out a happy bark. Thunder rumbled off in the distance, and Brave's ears flicked toward the sound. He furrowed his brow with worry, but kept his eyes on Dylan and his tail up.

"I wish he could tell us what happened to him while he was gone," Dylan said.

"You mean like talk about his feelings?" Grace grinned.

"Yeah, pretty much."

"I can tell you what my feelings are: I'll be very happy to get back on two wheels," Grace said as they stepped around large stones and tangled underbrush. "And on solid ground."

"Me too."

"Shhh—" Grace held up a hand to shush him.

"Brave, stop," Dylan said. The three of them stood still.

"What is that?" Grace asked.

Dylan strained his ears to pick up the sound—it was a low, steady whooshing. "Is that water?" he said.

"But I didn't see a stream or river on the way in, did you?" Grace asked.

Dylan shook his head. "Come on." He led them toward the sound, which grew louder and louder until they finally stumbled onto the edge of a churning stream.

"What is th—" Dylan started to ask Grace. He looked down at the wide, rushing current of water that suddenly blocked their path where there had been no water before.

Brave took one curious step toward it, stretching his snout forward, then decided he'd seen enough and scooted back to Dylan's side.

Dylan's brain felt scrambled for a second, like he was seeing things where they didn't belong, until all at once he realized what was happening.

"Grace—" Dylan began, but she already understood.

"Flash flood!" Grace said.

"In the creek bed—" Dylan said.

"All that rain . . . there was nowhere for it to go."

"Our bikes!" Dylan exclaimed.

"Oh no," Grace groaned, burying her face in her hands. "I'm sure they're gone by now."

"We're not far from where we left them—let's hurry," Dylan said. "Maybe they got saved somehow."

They rushed along the bank, keeping an eye on the water level. By Dylan's estimate, it had to be at least five feet deep, and it was still rising as rainwater streamed down from the hills around them. The rain had come down too fast, and the ground had been too parched and rocky to take it all in.

"It's right up here, I think," Dylan said, picturing the big rock they'd leaned their bikes on. Brave trotted along beside him. They had come around a curve in the stream when all of a sudden, the dog's whole demeanor changed. His head spun around and his ears swung forward and up.

Every muscle in his body went taut, and he stared off into the distance. He had heard something on a frequency that Dylan and Grace couldn't pick up.

"What is it, Brave?" Dylan asked.

"Shhhh." Grace focused her eyes on the ground as she strained her ears to hear what Brave had tuned in to.

Dylan tried too but heard nothing over the rush of the water. Brave was still on alert, though—and still listening carefully to something.

They stood there, tense and silent, until a sound floated toward them.

"Help!"

Dylan and Grace looked at each other. "Jaxon!" they said at the same time.

"Where is he?" Grace asked.

"I can't tell!" Dylan replied.

"Help! Can anyone hear me?" Jaxon's voice came again.

"That way!" Dylan said, pointing up ahead. But Brave was way ahead of him. He shot off along the creek's edge toward the sound of Jaxon's calls, so fast that he ripped his leash from Dylan's hand. Brave ran at full speed as Grace and Dylan trailed behind.

"Help, somebody!" Jaxon screamed.

"Jaxon!" Dylan responded. "Where are you?"

Dylan and Grace caught up to Brave just as he came screeching to a halt. Dylan's heart was pounding, and his chest hurt from running so hard. Brave paced back and forth along the water's edge, his muzzle pointed up to the sky as he barked into the air excitedly. He pawed at the ground in a skittering dance.

"Over here!" Jaxon called out.

Dylan followed the sound of his voice, toward the water. At the center of the torrent, atop the flat rock where they had left their bikes, stood Jaxon. But the rock was almost entirely submerged. The water had risen so high that it splashed over Jaxon's feet—and surrounded him on all sides.

Jaxon was trapped.

"Jaxon!" Dylan cried out. "Are you okay?"

"Help me!" Jaxon called to them. "I'm stuck!"

Brave's barking reached a fever pitch. He took a few running steps into the rapid current of the creek until he was up to his chest.

"Brave—no!" Dylan commanded him. Brave froze. "Come!" The dog splashed out of the water and snapped to Dylan's side. Dylan turned to Grace. "We have to get Jaxon out of there," he said.

"Yeah." Grace nodded, pressing her lips into a grim line. "But we also have to get ourselves out of here." She pointed at the water, which was now lapping at their toes. "It's still rising."

"We can't leave him here!" Dylan said.

"No, but if we get swept up in that, we're not going to be able to help him at all."

Flash floods were incredibly dangerous, Dylan knew. They lived in what people called Flash Flood Alley—where dry creeks and riverbeds could easily overflow when it rained too fast and hard. His parents had told him a thousand times that even a few inches of water moving that fast could knock him down and sweep him away. And this was way more than a few inches.

Dylan studied the water around Jaxon. It was fast-moving and rough, and it had swept up tons of debris in its path. He saw tree trunks and uprooted shrubbery and even a random rubber tire zip past.

It was dangerous, but he couldn't leave his friend out there in the middle of all that raging water.

At Dylan's side, Brave whimpered and pawed at the water's edge. He had his eyes locked on Jaxon, and he was shaking. Dylan dropped to his knees to comfort the dog.

"I know, buddy," Dylan said. "We're going to get Jaxon. And I know it's loud—you're doing great." Brave seemed to calm down at the sound of Dylan's voice. But the calming effect went both ways. Dylan wrapped his arms around Brave's neck and took a long, slow breath.

"Dylan?" Jaxon's voice shook. "Hurry." The water was up to his ankles.

Dylan stood up, and Brave leaned against his leg. "It's going to be okay," Dylan called to Jaxon, trying to keep his own voice steady. "We're going to get you out of there. Just give me a second to think."

"I don't know if I have a second, Dyl." Desperation rang through Jaxon's voice.

"You're going to be fine, Jax, I promise."

Dylan turned to Grace. "How do we get to him?" he asked.

Grace was chewing on her lip, her face screwed up with concentration. "We need some way to cross."

Just then, a long tree trunk swirled by on the surface of the water.

"I have an idea," Dylan said. It was risky, he knew, but it was the only choice they had. Dylan had made up his mind. He was going to save Jaxon, and he didn't care how dangerous it was. Because that's what friends did—they saved each other.

★ CHAPTER 24 ★

"Dylan, this is a bad idea," Grace said, one eye on the water at their feet. "This thing is getting higher by the second."

"We'll be quick." He looked upstream, squinting into the fading early-evening light. "There!" He pointed at a sheared-off tree branch that was speeding toward them. "Grab it!"

Dylan and Grace leaned over and snatched at opposite ends of the branch just as it reached them. They hauled it out of the water and dropped it at their feet, falling backward onto the muddy ground. Brave skittered around them, barking.

"Guys!" Jaxon called over. "What's happening?"

"Just hold on for me, okay, Jax?" Dylan replied. "We're coming."

"Now what?" Grace asked, standing up and wiping the dirt from her hands onto her jeans.

Dylan kicked at the narrow tree branch. "It's not wide enough," he said. "We need another one."

They positioned themselves by the water again and waited. It wasn't long before another hunk of wood was headed right for them. They leaned over and stretched out their arms. "Three," Dylan counted down. "Two. One—"

"Watch out!" Jaxon screamed from the rock. Dylan and Grace jumped back just in time to avoid a wildly spinning chunk of concrete that had broken off somewhere up river and come hurtling toward them on the surface of the water.

Dylan landed on his backside with a resounding thud, knocking the wind out of him again. Grace lay on her back next to him, breathing heavily. Brave licked Dylan's cheek, then turned to Grace and nudged her shoulder with his snout, as if to say *Get up!*

"Thanks," Dylan called to Jaxon.

"No problem," Jaxon replied.

"One more time," Grace said, getting to her feet again.

On the next try, they caught another long, solid tree branch and laid it down next to the first.

Dylan shook his head. "Still not enough," he said. Grace nodded, and they turned back to the water for one more.

Finally they had three strips of tree lying side by side. Together, they formed a surface wide enough to walk on

—but now Dylan and Grace had to somehow connect them to one another.

Grace pointed at Dylan's feet. "Your shoelaces," she said.

Dylan quickly pulled them out. "Good start," he said. "But they're not strong enough."

Grace thought for a moment. "Brave's leash!" she said. She unhooked it from his collar.

"Brave, sit," Dylan said firmly. Brave sat. "Stay." Brave ducked his head and stayed put.

Dylan tied the shoelaces together and used them to lash together one end of the log bridge. Grace wrapped the leash around the other end three times, then knotted it securely to itself. It was the best they were going to do under the circumstances.

"Now how do we get it over to him?" Grace asked.

Dylan had already thought that part through. "I'm going to wade out and lower it onto the rock."

"You can't do that, Dylan!" Her eyes were round with fear. "It's too dangerous!"

"What's our other choice?" Dylan asked. "He's got nowhere to go and the water's rising."

She shook her head. "I can't let you do this."

"You're not letting me. I'm choosing to."

She grimaced. "Are you sure this is going to work?"

Dylan wasn't going to lie to her. "Nope. But there's only one way to find out."

Grace covered her face with her hands and shook her head. "Ugh—fine," she exclaimed. "But please don't get hurt."

"I'll try not to if you'll try not to," Dylan said.

"Deal. Let's go."

They raised up one end and dragged the heavy logs over to the water's edge. Brave ran in loops around them, barking like he knew what they were thinking and wanted to talk them out of it.

"Ready?" Dylan said.

Grace nodded. She kneeled down and braced the end of the wooden structure that sat in the mud. Dylan lowered the other end toward the water. He stepped carefully into the rushing tide. The current was far stronger than he had imagined it could be. It wrapped itself around his ankles, then his calves, with a firm grasp, pushing and pulling him along with it. He wobbled under its pressure but managed to stay upright.

"Dylan—be careful!" Jaxon shouted.

"Hurry!" Grace yelled.

Dylan waded out as far as he dared, until the water reached his knees. From where he stood, he could only lower the wood to a foot or so above the rock—and then he would have to drop it.

"Watch out, Jax," Dylan said. "Step back."

With a grunt, Dylan let go and threw his arms out to the side to catch his balance. The wood slammed into the rock. For a second, he feared the strong current would knock it off. But it stayed put, forming a bridge directly from where Jaxon stood to the other side, where Grace beckoned to him. Still in the water, Dylan leaned against the log ramp, bracing it with his body against the powerful flood.

"Come on!" Grace shouted, waving her hands at Jaxon. "Cross over—quick!"

"Dude, let's go!" Dylan yelled. He wasn't sure how much longer he could hold the tree trunks—or himself—in place.

But Jaxon didn't respond. He was frozen in fear, transfixed by the churning water. "I can't." His voice cracked.

"Wait—what? No!" Dylan responded. "I mean yes, you can! You got this, Jaxon." He steadied his voice. "You're going to be fine . . . It's just like . . . it's just like . . . uh . . . walking on the sidewalk! No big deal. Come on now."

"It's okay, Jaxon!" Grace called out. "We're holding it still. We're not going to let you fall." She turned to Dylan. "What do we do?" she said loud enough that only Dylan could hear.

"I don't know." Dylan hoped he didn't seem as panicked as he felt. What if they couldn't get Jaxon to cross over?

They couldn't leave him there — could they? Should they go for help? What if they left him but when they came back . . . it was too late?

Dylan shook his head to clear it. His feet were aching from the cold water, and his legs were starting to shake.

"Jaxon, I need you to listen to me," Dylan said, his voice firm like he was giving Brave a command. "You just have to take the first step. And after that it'll be easy."

Jaxon squeezed his eyes shut and took a few steadying breaths. "Okay," he said. He opened them and stretched out his leg. Carefully, slowly, he put his toes on the wood, then the rest of his foot. He shifted his weight to lift up his other foot, and the whole thing wobbled.

"No!" Jaxon screamed, jumping back and almost slipping off the rock.

Before Dylan could utter a word, he saw a dark blur whip by out of the corner of his eye, headed right for the water.

It was Brave.

The dog leapt onto the bridge, which dipped under his weight. Dylan and Grace steadied it as best they could, and Brave was across it in a few graceful strides. He stood up on his hind legs and grabbed ahold of Jaxon's T-shirt with his teeth, then spun around to pull him across.

Jaxon had no choice — he either followed Brave or fell headfirst into the racing water. Too surprised to do anything but react, he did as Brave wanted him to. Jaxon put one foot down, then another, then the next.

Dylan watched nervously, biting his tongue so he wouldn't break the spell Jaxon seemed to be under. Soon, Jaxon was halfway across, and, for a split second, Dylan began to believe that his friend was going to make it. All thanks to Brave.

Then, as if it were happening in slow motion, he watched a horrible scene play frame by frame.

First, Brave released his hold on Jaxon's shirt and turned to face forward. Then, Jaxon's arms windmilled through the air as he started to lose his balance. His face contorted into a silent scream as his feet slipped on the wet wood, sliding out from under him. Brave spun around and snapped at the air with his jaw, trying to catch Jaxon, but it was too late.

With barely a splash, Jaxon was in the water. Then he disappeared beneath the surface before the scream could even leave Dylan's mouth.

"No!" Grace cried.

"Jaxon!" Dylan shouted.

Brave barked wildly, leaning out over the water, all the fur on his back standing on end. Dylan felt helpless. He couldn't dive in after his friend, because if he let go of the logs, then Brave would fall in too — and Jaxon would have nothing to hold on to when he came up again.

If he came up again.

Brave scurried back and forth across the ramp, then froze. He stared at a spot in the water that Dylan couldn't see, and every muscle in his body flexed. Dylan realized what Brave was about to do just as he did it—but it was too late to stop him. Brave pushed off his back legs, stretched his front paws out, hurled himself into the water, and was gone. Dylan frantically scanned the surface for any sign of his friend or his dog, but for an excruciating few seconds, there was nothing.

Behind him, Grace let out a strangled, fearful cry. Tears filled Dylan's eyes. Then, all of a sudden, Brave broke through the surface, paddling and kicking hard and pulling Jaxon by the sleeve. Jaxon took a huge gulp of air and flailed his hands around until he got ahold of the log bridge. He pulled himself up onto it as Brave scrambled up next to him, his claws scratching at the wood.

Dylan and Grace held their breath, and before they knew it, Brave and Jaxon had crawled across the ramp, over the water and onto slippery—but solid—ground.

They were safe.

Brave had saved Jaxon.

★ CHAPTER 25 ★

Just as Jaxon collapsed into the mud, coughing up water, Dylan and Grace let go of their makeshift bridge and watched it spiral away on the swift current.

Jaxon rolled onto his side and reached out a hand to Brave, who lay panting next to him. "Thank you, Brave," he said. Brave stretched out his snout and licked water off Jaxon's face, and Jaxon laughed out loud.

Dylan and Grace dropped to the ground next to him.

"That sucked," Dylan said.

"It really did," Grace said.

"But man, I'm glad you're okay," Dylan said to Jaxon.

Jaxon sat up and looked from Dylan to Grace and back again. "I'm so sorry," he said to them, his face twisted up like he was fighting to keep his composure. "I was wrong —so wrong. About everything."

"Wellll . . ." Dylan said. "You're not entirely wrong there."

"I never should have shot off those fireworks," Jaxon continued. "You told me it was a bad idea, but I didn't listen. And I didn't mean to scare Brave—he's an awesome dog. I'm sorry I made him run away. He—" Jaxon swallowed hard. "He saved my life," he managed to choke out. "You all did. Thank you."

Dylan let Jaxon's words sink in. It had been so long since he'd seen this side of his friend—for a second it was like a time warp or something. *This* was who Jaxon really was. This was who Dylan had been missing all along. And this was the person he wanted Grace to know.

"Apology accepted," Dylan said. He turned to Grace, as if to say *See—he's not so bad!*

"But you have been treating Dylan really badly," Grace piped in. "Can you promise you'll stop?"

"It's okay, Gra—" Dylan started to say.

"No, Dyl." Jaxon held up a hand to interrupt him. "She's right. I'm sorry for the way I've been treating you. And I will stop. I promise. It's just that . . ." He looked guiltily at Grace, then back at Dylan. "We started middle school and you made a new friend and suddenly had Brave and the ranch and I just felt . . . left out. I was jealous. Like you were moving on without me." Jaxon looked down at the ground. "I don't blame you for hating me."

"I don't hate you," Dylan said. "And I'm not moving

on, I'm just . . . I don't know . . ." He searched for the right word. "Expanding. Plus I felt like you were moving on, too."

"I'm not!" Jaxon said. "Maybe I'm expanding too."

"That's a good thing," Dylan replied.

"Soooo," Jaxon said, "if you're not moving on, and I'm not moving on, then we can still be friends, right?"

Dylan studied Jaxon's remorseful face for a second. "Jax," Dylan said softly. "I'll always be your friend. I just don't always want to do some of the stuff you want to do. But I'm not going anywhere."

"You mean it?"

"Yeah, I mean it."

"Awesome," Jaxon said with a weary smile.

★ ★ ★

Their bikes were long gone, so they plodded along through the twilight on foot. As soon as they got back into cell phone range, they texted their parents to say they were safe, on their way home . . . and very, very sorry. Their parents replied with a variety of choice words, but mostly relief.

The storm clouds continued to break, and stars began to appear one by one and twinkle overhead. Dylan paused and looked up, letting his relief and a wave of exhaustion wash over him.

They'd done it. They'd saved Brave and were taking him home.

Grace and Jaxon stopped to look up too. Just then, Brave froze on the path ahead of them, and his ears swung forward on his head. He fixated on a spot in the underbrush, and a low growl escaped his throat. Dylan heard rustling in the leaves followed by a lot of frantic squeaking. A rodent of some kind was probably packing up its whole family and plotting an escape at the sight of the dog.

"Brave, come," Dylan said. With a longing look at the bushes, Brave obeyed the command and trotted over to Dylan's side.

"That's amazing," Jaxon said. "He's so well trained."

"That's Grace," Dylan replied. "She taught me how to teach Brave."

"You did all the work," Grace said.

"Grace . . ." Jaxon said. "Nice job. Dylan told me you're really good with animals."

Grace shrugged. "I've just grown up with them, that's all. And Brave's a great dog." She looked at Jaxon, and for the first time in Dylan's memory, she wasn't shooting daggers at him with her eyes. In fact, he thought he saw her almost smile. "But thanks," she said to Jaxon.

As he watched Grace's expression soften and Jaxon finally say something nice for once, Dylan felt a burst of hope. He could picture the two of them maybe, just maybe, getting along. Then he let himself entertain an even crazier thought that would have seemed impossible only a few hours earlier: What if his oldest friend and his newest friend actually really *liked* each other? What if they could all hang out together?

He couldn't imagine anything better.

Just then, Brave stuffed his snout into Dylan's palm, looking for a pat.

Unless, Dylan thought as he ran a thumb over the dog's forehead, *Brave is there too.*

★ CHAPTER 26 ★

Dylan had never been so happy to see his front yard before. It was night by the time he, Brave, Grace, and Jaxon finally made their way back home. The bedraggled crew stopped outside Dylan's house.

Dylan turned to the others. "See you at school tomorrow?"

Jaxon groaned. "Ugh. I forgot it was a school night."

"Assuming I'm not so grounded I can't even go to school," Grace said. "I'm so late. I have to go."

"Good night," Dylan said. "Thank you so much, Grace."

She nodded and shot him a small smile. "You're welcome, Dylan. You'll make it up to me when you clear twice as much land tomorrow."

His face lit up. "I can come back to the ranch?"

"Like I said—if you clear twice as much land, you can."

"Deal."

"Night, Jaxon," Grace said.

Dylan held his breath.

"Night, Grace." Jaxon said. "Thanks for . . . you know. Everything."

"You're welcome," she said, then paused. "I know we haven't always agreed on things, but I'm really glad we're friends. I just wanted to say that. And, um, you're both officially Ranch Kids now, whether you like it or not."

Dylan laughed as Jaxon made a face. "Fine," Jaxon said. "But that means you have to be in our water balloon fights every weekend now."

"You got it," Grace said with a smirk. "And I'm going to win."

All of a sudden, Grace stepped forward and hugged Jaxon, then Dylan. Shock radiated through Dylan's system, but he hugged her back. Part of him wanted to play it cool —even though he could sense that something was different between himself and Grace, not just between Grace and Jaxon. It was as if they were becoming real friends.

With a final wave goodbye, Grace headed down the road back to her house.

"You were right about her," Jaxon said once Grace was out of earshot. "The same way you were right about Brave." At the sound of his name, Brave trotted over to Jaxon, stood up on his hind legs, and put his front paws on Jaxon's leg. "Yeah, I'm talking about you," Jaxon said, giving Brave a couple of good solid scratches behind the ears. Brave wagged his tail and let out a contented yip.

"Well, I better go in and face my mom," Dylan said. "Night, Jax."

"Night, Dyl."

Dylan shut the back door quietly behind him, but his mom was in the kitchen in an instant.

"Oh, thank God you're okay!" She wrapped him in a huge hug as Brave hopped all around her legs, as excited to see her as she was to see Dylan. "Are you okay?"

"Yes—I'm fine, Mom. I'm so sorry—"

She pulled away and Dylan saw that she had her phone to her ear. "He's here, honey—I know. I know. Brave's here too." She wiped a tear from the corner of her eye and pointed at the phone, mouthing *your dad* to Dylan. "Yes. I'll tell him. No, he looks okay." She sized up Dylan—soaking wet, slathered in dirt and mud, twigs in his hair, no shoelaces —and shook her head. "I think he has a lot to tell us about where he's been. But don't worry. I'll punish him enough for both of us. I'll have him call you later. Love you—bye."

"Mom—you won't believe—"

She cut him off. "We were about to send out a search party for you! Do you have any idea how scared we were? And Dad is so far away, he felt so helpless—oh, come here." She pulled him into another hug, so tight she squeezed the air out of his lungs. "I'm so happy to see you, honey. Please don't ever do that to us again or I will not survive it."

"I'm sorry, Mom. I really am." Dylan felt terrible for scaring his parents so badly. But he really wanted to tell her about Brave, about how amazing the dog had been.

His mom went to get two towels, one for him and one for Brave. Dylan wrapped himself in one, dried the dog off with the other, then collapsed onto the couch. Brave jumped up next to him, spun around three times, and lay down. Within seconds, Brave was sound asleep and snoring.

"Now. Tell me what happened," his mom said, sitting down on the other side of Brave.

Dylan took a deep breath. And then he started at the beginning—with the cowboy hat, and Grace storming out of the classroom, and the fireworks . . . As he told his mom the story, the reality of what he and Brave and his friends had just been through began to fully hit him.

"Brave saved Jaxon's life, Mom," Dylan said, his voice breaking. "He's amazing—I wish you could have seen him. You have no idea how . . . well, *brave* he really is. I didn't know what we were going to do, but he did." Brave woke up and raised his head, squinted at Dylan—as if checking to make sure Dylan was okay—then dropped his head onto Dylan's lap and closed his eyes again. "He wasn't even scared by the noise of the water or anything. It was like he just . . . I don't know . . . like he just did what he had to do."

Dylan's mom rubbed Brave behind the ears with both hands, and he let out a sleepy, happy grunt. "You did good, Brave. I'm so thankful you were there to help the kids."

She turned to Dylan, and he could tell by the look on her face that there was a big *but* coming.

"But," his mom said, her voice serious, "Dylan, you understand that Brave is also the reason you were out there in the first place?"

Dylan saw where she was headed, and he wanted to change her mind. "I was out there because I made a bad decision to go with Jaxon," he said quickly.

"Well, yes, and that's something we're going to need to discuss, honey. But I mean that you had to go after Brave because he got scared by the fireworks and ran away. And it's not just the fireworks or loud sounds. He's unpredictable, and he's a flight risk. I know you were trying to do your best, but you made a really dangerous choice out there. You can't just chase after him every time. You're safe today, but what about next time?"

The lump in Dylan's throat stopped him from answering.

"I agree that Brave is a special dog, but I'm afraid he also has some really serious issues." She let her words sink in for a second. "Grace has been amazing—I can see how much progress you guys have made. But it's better for Brave if he gets real training. By an expert. Otherwise he's going to keep putting you in bad situations, and that's not something I'm willing to accept."

Dylan's heart plunged into his stomach.

"What are you saying, Mom?" he managed to utter. "Are you telling me I have to say goodbye to him for good?"

She smiled. "No, honey—not for good. I'm saying that we're going to find the best help possible for Brave, so that you *won't* have to say goodbye. I found a trainer who specializes in helping dogs learn to cope with their stress. And, believe it or not, she's willing to help him for a really low fee because he's a hurricane dog. He's going to go and live with her."

"Live with her?" Dylan couldn't fight it—his eyes filled with tears. "You mean, he can't stay here while he gets trained?"

She put a hand on Dylan's arm. "It's only for a little while, honey, and if—*if*—Brave can get past this, then he'll come back and you can keep him. We can keep him."

"Really?"

"Really."

"He can do it, Mom—I know he can!" Dylan pumped both fists in the air. "Thanks, Mom!" He leaned across

Brave and threw his arms around her, squishing the dog in the process. Brave rolled onto his back and kicked at Dylan's stomach with his back legs. "Oh, sorry, boy." Dylan sat up again. "But did you hear that? You're going to get trained, and then you can stay!"

Brave stretched all four paws in the air and let Dylan and his mom rub his belly.

"You're going to do great," Dylan said. In response, the dog threw his head back and yowled. Dylan and his mom burst out laughing. "But first, boy," Dylan said, wrinkling his nose, "you need a serious bath. You stink."

"I'll call your father back while you take care of that," his mom said.

"Follow me, Brave." Dylan led him down the hall. With a yawn, Brave walked straight into the bathroom and hopped into the tub on Dylan's command.

For the first time since he'd found Brave in that alley, hiding behind a dumpster, Dylan was filled with hope that they could — and would — be together forever.

★ CHAPTER 27 ★

He'd known this day was coming for a week, but that didn't seem to make it any easier. It was time to say goodbye to Brave.

Dylan sat up in bed and stared out the window. In a couple of hours, he and his mom would drive Brave to a kennel outside the city, where Brave would live for the foreseeable future. There was no telling how long it would be—it might be a couple of weeks or a few months. But the good news was that no one had claimed Brave at the shelter, so if Dylan's parents agreed, they could officially adopt Brave when he came back.

The trainer his mom had found was known as the best in the region, and she'd helped many other dogs who'd been traumatized by hurricanes or other big, scary events. Brave would be comfortable—he'd have a few acres to roam and run freely, and lots of other dogs to keep him company.

He'd be well taken care of, and Dylan would get to visit on the weekends to see Brave's progress. But Brave wasn't the only one who would have to work hard. Dylan would be expected to train with Brave when he was there visiting.

This was what would be best for Brave—Dylan knew that. Then why did it still hurt so much to say goodbye?

Brave was sound asleep at the foot of Dylan's bed, his paws twitching like he was chasing a squirrel in a dream. Dylan kicked off the covers and flipped over on his bed, lying on his stomach with his face next to Brave's.

"Morning, buddy," he said. Brave opened one eye and stared at him. He opened his mouth to yawn, letting out a squeaky yowl and a blast of warm dog breath right onto Dylan's face. "Delicious," Dylan groaned.

He sat up and took Brave's head in his hands. They stared at each other for a minute.

"Listen," Dylan said. "We're going to take you somewhere today, and you're probably going to wonder why I'm leaving you there." He felt a sharp pang—would Brave think he was abandoning him? "But it's just temporary, okay? And you're going to work really hard, and I'm going to come see you as much as I can, and then we're going to be together again."

Brave put one paw on Dylan's arm and nuzzled Dylan's cheek with his cool wet nose. Dylan thought back to Brave running over the slippery logs, pulling Jaxon by the shirt, and diving into the dark, churning water to save him — and he knew everything was going to be okay.

"All you need to do," he said, smiling down at the dog, "is be brave."

★ ★ ★

Dylan didn't speak for the entire car ride. He sat in the back so he could spend every last second with Brave, who had his head on his lap. Dylan absentmindedly stroked the dog's ears and ran his fingers through the smooth fur around his neck.

His phone dinged in his pocket. It was a text from his dad.

I know it's a tough day but I'm proud of you.

Thanks dad, Dylan texted back.

This is what's best for Brave and the family, his dad wrote.

I know. But I'm going to miss him.

Yeah. I know what it's like to miss someone you love.

Ha. Funny. Love you.

Love you too.

When they got to the kennel, a tall, smiling woman greeted them at the front.

"I'm Amelia." She gave Dylan's hand a firm shake. "You must be Dylan. And you" — she turned to the dog — "are definitely Brave." She held out a hand for Brave to investigate with a good sniff. "We're going to get along great. Sit," she said in a clear, strong voice. Brave sat, and she gave him a treat from a small bag hanging from her hip. "Good boy."

Something about her demeanor comforted Dylan. Amelia was warm and friendly, but firm—in charge. He knew in his gut that Brave would be in good hands.

"So, Dylan," Amelia said, after she'd led them on a tour of the spotless facility and back to their car. "I want you to know that I will care for Brave as if he were my dog. But—" She stopped and turned to him for emphasis. "He's not here on vacation. He's going to be working very hard, and I have high expectations for him. It's a hard road for dogs with serious trauma, and he's got a lot of learning to do."

Dylan nodded. "I know. He can handle it."

"Well, he's already off to a great start."

"He is?" Dylan asked.

Amelia smiled and put a hand on his shoulder. "He really is. You did a great job training him—especially for someone who has never had a dog before. I can tell already that he's bonded with you, which is so important and will make all the difference in his training. And he wants to do a good job. That's half the battle right there."

"So you think he has a shot?" Dylan asked.

"I do," Amelia said. "Thanks to you."

Relief washed over Dylan. He dropped to his knees

and held Brave's head in his hands. The look of fear and confusion in the dog's eyes nearly broke Dylan's heart. He wrapped his arms around Brave's neck, and Brave leaned into him, as if he knew that this was goodbye, at least for a little while.

"You got this, buddy," Dylan whispered into Brave's ear. "I know you do. I'll see you really soon, okay?"

Dylan held on for just one more second. Then he forced himself to stand up, turn away, and get in the car—leaving Brave behind.

★ ★ ★

The night sky rumbled like a drum. Dylan wrapped his sweatshirt snugly around himself and pulled his knees into his chest. They had just finished dinner, and he and his mom were sitting together on the porch, waiting for the rain to start.

The first day without Brave had been strange—Dylan kept thinking he saw the dog out of the corner of his eye, but when he turned to look, nothing was there. They hadn't even had Brave for very long, but already Dylan had gotten so used to him, like he'd always been a part of their household. Dylan could tell his mom was surprised by the stillness and quiet too.

He peered up at the dark sky just as a bolt of lightning

flashed. Then he counted the seconds until the thunder began again.

"Do you think he's okay—I mean, with the thunder?"

"I think Amelia will make sure he is," his mom replied.

"What if he's scared right now?" Just the thought of it made Dylan's chest ache. He wanted desperately to get back in the car, drive out to the kennel, and bring his dog home —where he could protect him.

"He might be. But that's why he's there—to get the help he needs."

"I know. But still."

"It's hard to be separated from the ones you love." His mom sighed. Dylan couldn't see her face in the dark, but he thought he heard a note of sadness in her voice.

Dylan thought back to the day his dad had left a few months earlier. He was used to his dad coming and going —he'd been in the military since before Dylan was born. But that didn't mean it got easier to say goodbye. In fact, in some ways, it got harder as Dylan got older, because there was more to miss—more fun stuff that they liked to do together, more real conversations, more family traditions, more laughs.

Dylan suddenly felt awful that he'd never thought to ask his mom how she felt about his dad being gone. He'd always been so focused on how much he missed him. He'd never realized before how hard it must be for his mom to be alone so much of the time.

"Do you miss Dad a lot?"

"Yeah," she said simply. "I do."

"Me too," Dylan said.

"But, Dylan, your dad always comes home. And Brave is going to come home too, you know," his mom said, as if she could read his mind.

"I hope so."

"I know so."

Just then, one giant crack of thunder wrenched open the clouds, and the rain came pouring down. Dylan and his mom jumped to their feet and scrambled inside. Dylan kissed his mom good night and headed upstairs, thinking about what she had said.

★ CHAPTER 28 ★

Brave and Dylan had been apart longer than they'd been together. Four long weeks had gone by, but Dylan was doing his best to focus on the good: Brave was a star student, according to Amelia. Not only was he getting better trained by the day, but he was gradually getting less scared too.

Dylan had been out to train with them every weekend, and he was amazed at how much Brave had learned. He was still his same sweet, happy self, but Dylan noticed that something about Brave had changed—he was sharp and alert, and he followed commands with precision. It was like he was becoming the dog he was always meant to be.

The last time he was there, though, Amelia had said she still wasn't sure when Brave would be ready to come home. Dylan was trying so hard to be patient, but he could barely wait until Brave greeted him at the door every day after school and rolled around in the dirt on the ranch with Mustang.

Mustang, who at that moment was chasing a bee that flew in wide swoops around the field. Dylan stopped to watch her prancing around, her mouth open and her tail wagging.

"Taking a break there, Dyl?"

"Dude—seriously?" Dylan took off his cowboy hat, wiped the sweat from his forehead, and shot Jaxon a look. "You're one to talk."

"Oh, like you're moving so fast?" Jaxon replied.

"Faster than you!" Dylan pointed at the meager stack of new fence posts behind Jaxon.

"Guys, stop fighting," Grace said. "You're both slow."

Judging by the neat, tall pyramid of wooden posts behind her, she was right. Dylan and Jaxon looked at each other and couldn't help but crack up.

"Race you," Jaxon said.

"You're on." Dylan and Jaxon ran to the truck side by side, jostling each other out of the way as they pulled new posts off the flatbed. Mustang nipped at their heels, herding them.

"Is that all it takes to motivate you two slowpokes?" Grace rolled her eyes. "A little friendly competition?"

"Yup." Dylan grunted as he carried one heavy slab of wood over each shoulder.

"Who said it was friendly?" Jaxon shoved past Dylan, carrying an armful.

"You should get grounded more often," Grace said to Jaxon. "We'd get a lot more done around here."

Jaxon's parents had not been pleased about the incident with the fireworks and the watermelon. They were all set to ground him—for a very long time—when Jaxon proposed a different plan, which he and Dylan had hatched together. Jaxon persuaded them to let him work on the ranch every day after school instead of keeping him in the house. It would not only teach him a valuable lesson, but it would also help out Grace and her family.

Dylan's mom thought that was a great idea and decided Dylan could work off his poor choices too. Their parents had made a plan with Grace's dad, and the boys had spent the last month helping Grace. So far they'd finished clearing debris from the field and rebuilt three-quarters of a fence that seemed to go on forever. Dylan was seeing fence posts in his dreams at night, but he didn't mind. He was asleep by the time his head hit the pillow anyway.

Plus it was a good way to pass the time—with his two best friends—while he waited for Brave to come home.

Dylan heard the hum of a car engine and turned toward the road that wound its way through the ranch. He pulled the brim of his hat down to shade his eyes and recognized his mom's car. Why was she coming to get him?

The car pulled to a stop nearby, and the back window rolled down. Dylan gasped when he saw who was in the back seat. A familiar bluish-gray figure stuck his head through the window, his amber eyes sparkling, his tongue dangling from his mouth, and his ears perked up.

"Brave!" all three kids shouted at once.

Brave stood up and wagged his tail, practically vibrating with excitement. He swiped a paw in the air and ducked his head, as if to say *Let me out of here.* Dylan dropped the fence posts to the ground and ran over to him, expecting Brave to jump through the window to meet him. But Brave didn't move. Instead he just watched Dylan, his eyes filled with anticipation.

He was waiting for a command. Dylan couldn't believe it.

"Come here, buddy!" he called, spreading out his arms in greeting. Brave hopped out the window and landed lightly on his feet, then ran to Dylan. Normally, Brave would have jumped all over him in greeting, but he didn't. He just wagged his tail and looked up at Dylan with his tongue out and a happy grin on his face. Brave looked poised, calm, confident.

"What are you doing here?" Dylan asked, dropping to

his knees and wrapping his arms around Brave's neck in a big hug. He let Brave lick his face from top to bottom, not even caring that the dog was slobbering all over him.

Dylan looked up at the car, expecting his mom to get out. Instead, the passenger-side door opened, and someone unfolded himself from the seat. Then everything happened so fast—Dylan was up on his feet, his feet were off the ground, and he was being wrapped in an enormous bear hug.

"Dad?" Dylan's voice was muffled as it pressed into his dad's shoulder.

"Dylan—oh, man, am I happy to see you!" he heard his dad say.

Dylan hugged him back as tightly as he could.

"What are you doing here?" Dylan asked. "You weren't supposed to come back for another week!"

"I wanted to surprise you."

"I can't believe it's really you." A million thoughts exploded in Dylan's head at once, and he thought his chest might burst with that special combination of joy and sadness that he felt every time his dad came home. Not that Dylan and his mom weren't okay when he was gone—they were. But when his dad returned from deployment, it was like Dylan's whole world shifted a little, into the proper position. When they were all together, everything was right again.

There was so much he wanted to tell his dad, so much he wanted to show him, but Dylan could only get one sentence out. "I missed you so much," he said, his voice cracking.

"I missed you so much too, pal. You have no idea." His dad set him on the ground and held Dylan at arm's length so he could take him in. "Look at you! You've grown a few inches for sure."

Dylan felt something scratching at his leg—Brave! There was only one thing that could be better than his dad coming home: his dad and Brave coming home at the same time.

"So you met Brave?" Dylan said.

"I did," his dad replied. "We've been getting to know each other in the car. He's a pretty great dog, Dyl. You were right about him."

Dylan's mom got out of the driver's seat. "Surprise!" she said, holding her palms up by her shoulders.

His parents enveloped him in a family hug while Grace and Jaxon watched. After a moment, Dylan's dad raised his head and beckoned them over.

"Get in here, Jax," he said. "And you must be Grace."

"Nice to meet you, sir," Grace said.

"I hear you've been a great help to Dylan," his dad said. "Thank you."

"It was nothing," Grace said, though she looked pleased.

"Group hug!" Dylan's mom said, wrapping an arm around Grace's shoulders and pulling her in.

Dylan had never felt so happy in his entire life. He looked around the huddle, at each of the people who meant so much to him. His parents beamed at him. *Thank you*, he mouthed to his mom. She winked.

Brave wedged his way into the center of the group.

"Bring it in, buddy!" Dylan laughed. Then a thought occurred to him. "Wait, Mom — is Brave just here for today, or is he home for good?"

"He's home for good," his mom said. "And," she added with a huge smile, "Amelia said he's the best dog she's ever worked with."

"Really?" Dylan asked, astonished.

"Really. She said he got a great start with you and Grace, and it only got better and better from there."

Dylan sat down on the ground so he was at Brave's level. He scratched the back of the dog's head, and Brave let out a snort of satisfaction. He wagged his tail wildly.

"I knew you could do it," Dylan said to Brave.

"We could say the same for you, Dyl," his mom said. "Your dad and I are so proud of both of you."

"There's something else, Dylan," his dad said, his voice suddenly serious. "Something your mom and I wanted to tell you together."

"What?" Dylan felt a spike of worry, until his dad broke out into a huge grin.

"Brave's not the only one who's home for good. I am too."

"What?" Dylan screamed so loud his parents covered their ears and laughed.

"And now," his dad said, "we can start the rest of our lives together as a family. All four of us."

"I can't wait," Dylan said. "Did you hear that, Brave? Dad's home forever—just like you!" Brave slurped Dylan's cheek in response.

Grace dropped to her knees at Brave's side. "Welcome back, buddy," she said.

Jaxon got down too and held out a hand to the dog. Brave sniffed it, then took a step forward and sniffed Jaxon's face. Brave exhaled sharply into Jaxon's eye, which Jaxon took as a good sign. "That means I passed some kind of test, right?"

"Sure." Dylan laughed. "Let's go with that." He pulled Brave in close, resting his head against the dog's. "I'm so happy you're back." Dylan sighed.

Grace wrapped an arm around the dog from the other side. "You're here to stay, Brave," she said, tipping her head to his.

"You know what this calls for, right?" Jaxon asked.

"Uh-oh—what?" Dylan groaned.

"Dog pile!" Jaxon shouted, raising both fists in the air in a triumphant cheer. "Woooooooohooooo!"

The sound of Dylan, Grace, and Jaxon's laughter rose up into the sky high above the ranch, catching the wind and mixing with Brave's happy howls.

★ ALL ABOUT THE BLUE LACY ★

★ Lacy dogs are fast, energetic, and hard-working dogs who love to have a purpose and really need a job — like herding cattle and game animals many times their size.

★ Lacys are a breed of working dogs developed in Texas beginning in the mid-nineteenth century. The original breed mixture is credited to the Lacy brothers — Frank, George, Edwin, and Harry — who moved from Kentucky to Texas in 1858. According to the Lacy family, the first Lacy dog was a mixture of English shepherd, greyhound, wolf, and possibly coyote. The Lacy brothers were trying to breed the perfect herding dog for their free-roaming hogs.

★ Lacy dogs are fast, lightly built dogs that have an intense work ethic. They are exceptional trackers, herders, and hunters who are energetic enough to contain even large game and livestock. Lacy dogs need to be kept occupied in order to be happy, which makes them great ranch dogs—and extremely popular in Texas. Lacys have often been used to find lost livestock as well as for hunting. A Lacy dog who doesn't have true "work" can be kept busy and happy with agility training.

★ The average female Lacy dog weighs between twenty-five and forty-five pounds, while males are usually thirty-five to fifty-five pounds. Lacy dogs come in a variety of colors, although many people refer to the entire breed as Blue Lacy.

★ Lacy dogs come in three colors. Blue Lacys are the most well-known and sought-after of the Lacy dogs. They have beautiful, eye-catching fur that appears blue-gray and ranges in shade from slate to silvery-black. Red Lacy dogs can range from light beige to a dark, deep red. And tricolored Lacy dogs are blue with red and white markings.

★ The Lacy dog was recognized by the Texas legislature in 2001 as a "true Texas breed." In 2005, the governor signed a document making the Blue Lacy the official state dog breed of Texas. When the mascot of Texas A&M University passed away in 2008, many rallied for the Blue Lacy to become the well-known symbol, but the university decided to stick with the collie, a breed they'd been using for years.

★ Lacy dogs do best when treated like a member of a team, rather than a family pet. Their herding instinct and high energy can make them too much for small children to handle. A Lacy dog needs firm direction and focus. They aren't necessarily friendly with other dogs and they may not respond well to cats or other small animals.

★ Lacy dogs require minimal grooming and have sleek, tight fur. They do shed, but not excessively, and they tend to be a healthy breed. Their life span is twelve to sixteen years.

★ Lacy dogs are one of the most intelligent, trainable dog breeds around. If given a job that engages them, they will flourish and be a devoted working companion. Lacy dogs are loyal and don't quit until the job is done.

A huge variety of both purebred and mixed-breed dogs are available for adoption from your local pet rescue. It is important to think carefully about how your family will care for and interact with a dog, so you can choose a breed that's just right for your household. If you have questions about whether a certain type of dog is right for you, contact a local veterinarian or your local rescue, or do a thorough Internet search to find the dog that would fit best with your family. This helps keep more dogs from returning to shelters and will help you enjoy a lifetime of happiness with your pet.

★ ACKNOWLEDGMENTS ★

Dogs rule. But if you have to be around humans, you couldn't do better than these folks: Emilia Rhodes, Catherine Onder, and the sales, marketing, and publicity teams at HMH. Les Morgenstein, Josh Bank, Sara Shandler, Romy Golan, and Laura Barbiea at Alloy Entertainment. Robin Straus, Katelyn Hales, Allen Zadoff, and my book better half, Hayley Wagreich. Thank you all!

Thank you to the people who love and feed me, and give me the occasional treat: Brian, the goons, Virginia Wing, Kunsang Bhuti, Tenzin Dekyi, and Vida (who is not a person, but who made the list on cuteness alone).

Turn the page for a preview of

★ CHAPTER 1 ★

Hannah pretended to study the rows of bagged salad mix and baby spinach as another shopper pushed a cart past her. She felt more than saw the man's eyes on her as he walked by. She kept the right side of her face turned away, her long, straight brown hair falling across her cheek like a curtain. She wished her mom would hurry up and finish picking out produce. She wanted to be back in her room, away from all the eyes turned in her direction.

It wasn't that people hadn't stared at Hannah in Michigan—they had. But her friends and teachers never treated her any differently because of the blotchy, reddish-purple birthmark that covered almost half of her face. Her friends had made it easier to ignore the sneaked glances and curious stares of strangers. But ever since her family had moved to California, the stares felt heavy and uncomfortable.

"Hannah, come see these avocados!" her mom exclaimed.

"We had avocados in Michigan," Hannah muttered to the spinach.

"Yes, but not like these." Her mom wrapped an arm around her shoulders and steered Hannah over to a pyramid of fruit. "We'll make guacamole. You love guacamole. It'll be even better because these are local!"

Her mom's voice had skipped into its too-cheerful tone, which had happened a lot since they'd moved to Deerwood. She kept saying things like *This is just like your favorite thing, only better!*

Except everything was worse here.

Hannah used to love making guacamole with her best friend, Linnea. They'd mash a big bowl of it, then sit on the living room floor with a bag of those tortilla chips in the shape of tiny little scoops. They'd eat the whole bowl while they watched movies. Local avocados wouldn't make up for her friend — for *all* of her friends — being so far away.

The scene her mom was making over the avocados was drawing even more stares.

"Okay, fine," Hannah said. "Can we just go?"

Hannah had wanted to stay home and hide with a book among the huge trees behind their house, away from the crying twins. But as soon as her dad returned from dropping her little sister off at soccer camp and the twins had gone down for their nap, her mom had decided they needed mother-daughter bonding time. Being dragged across town just to go to Safeway for groceries wasn't Hannah's idea of bonding, even with her mom's promise that they could stop for ice cream on the boardwalk on the way home.

Her mom's excitement slipped into a frown. But before she could say anything to Hannah about her attitude, another woman approached them.

"Oh, hi there!" The woman sounded extra friendly, just like everyone else who made a point of introducing themselves to the new family in town. "You live in the yellow ranch house on Cedar Drive, right?"

"That's us." Hannah's mom returned the woman's warm smile.

"I'm Dana Lin," she said. "We live in the blue two-story around the corner."

"I wasn't expecting to meet any of our neighbors in the produce aisle," Hannah's mom said.

Mrs. Lin laughed. "Well, it's not a farmers' market day."

"I'm Lila Carson," Hannah's mom said. "This is my daughter Hannah—my oldest."

"Hi!" Hannah said, forcing herself to sound as perky and nice as Mrs. Lin had. Her parents had always told her that being polite was the first step to helping people look past her birthmark.

Mrs. Lin turned toward Hannah for the first time, and

her smile fell into a look of surprise mixed with a little bit of pity—and a lot of questions. Like most adults, she recovered quickly. "It's so nice to meet you, Hannah. What grade are you in?"

"I'll be starting sixth," Hannah said.

"That's my daughter's grade." She took her eyes off Hannah's face to scan the produce section. "Sophia, come over here!"

A girl who'd been standing by the strawberries, typing on her phone, walked toward them without glancing up. She was slightly taller than Hannah, with long, thick black hair tied back in a loose ponytail. Her skin was clear and tan from the summer sun, with a dusting of tiny freckles across her nose.

"Sophia, these are our new neighbors," Mrs. Lin said. "Hannah will be in your class this year."

Sophia slowly looked up from her phone, her lips curving into a smile as she started to say hello. But when her gaze landed on Hannah, she froze, her mouth slightly open.

Heat crept up Hannah's face as Sophia stared. She knew that blushing only made her birthmark worse. Now her whole face was probably blotchy, instead of just the ragged patch that looked like a stain spreading from her chin to her eyebrow.

Hannah wished she could hide behind the avocados.

She didn't want to have to explain that she had been born with it and it would never go away. She didn't want to have to see how long it would take this girl with perfect skin to get used to looking at her—let alone get to know her. She wasn't sure if Sophia would even try.

She knew she should ask Sophia about school or at least say it was nice to meet her. But her tongue lay like a fat marshmallow in her mouth.

"We should all get together back in the neighborhood," Mrs. Lin said a little too brightly. "How old are your other kids?"

"Jenny is eight. And my twin boys are eighteen months."

"Wow, you have your hands full! Sophia has a younger sister too, so it'll be perfect."

"Sounds great," Hannah's mom said. "Hannah hasn't really met anyone since we moved here."

Embarrassment flared across Hannah's cheeks again. She tried to hide behind her hair, but it was too late. Sophia was back on her phone. She was probably telling all the other kids in their class about the new girl with the stained face and no friends.

"Why don't you all come over for brunch on Saturday?" Hannah's mom said.

Hannah flashed her a look, but her mom didn't notice.

"We'd love to," Mrs. Lin said.

★ ★ ★

"This is exciting," Hannah's mom said after Sophia and Mrs. Lin had headed toward the bread aisle. "You haven't had a playdate since we moved here."

"Mom, no one has playdates anymore," Hannah grumbled. She dreaded a whole morning of Sophia staring at her over pancakes.

"You know what I mean." Her mom sighed. "You've hardly left the house all summer."

"Well, on the upside, I haven't gotten a single sunburn this year."

Hannah thought she'd get a lecture on putting herself out in the world, but her mom was distracted by a display of tortillas. The avocados must have inspired her to make tacos for dinner. Normally, Hannah would have been excited about taco night, but just then she heard Sophia and her mom talking down the next aisle.

"It's hard to be the new kid in town," Mrs. Lin said. "You can still see your friends later in the afternoon."

"But what's wrong with her face?" Sophia asked.

Her mom shushed her. "Don't be rude."

Their voices faded as they walked away. Tears stung Hannah's eyes. The noises of the grocery store rose and fell around her—cash registers dinged and shopping carts clanged together. But even surrounded by the steady hum and buzz of the store, she felt lonely—separate from everyone around her, trapped behind the stain on her face.

Hannah missed her friends. They knew that the birthmark was just one small part of who she really was.

"Can we please go?" she asked quietly.

Her mom tossed a package of tortillas into the cart and turned to look at her. Hannah didn't think she'd heard what Sophia said, but her mom saw the tears in her eyes. "Oh, honey. It always takes time to make new friends."

"Jenny already has friends," Hannah said, thinking about how her younger sister had it so easy.

"It's different when you're little." Her mom brushed the hair back from Hannah's birthmark. "You'll see. Once people get to know you, it'll be even better than before."

Hannah pulled away from her mom. It was easy for her parents to say how great everything would be here. It had been their decision to move to some little town, a random dot dropped along the map of the California coastline. And they didn't have people constantly asking what was wrong with them.

★ CHAPTER 2 ★

Hannah sat on the giant Adirondack chair on the front porch, her legs tucked under her. Between texts to Linnea and rounds of *Candy Crush*, she glanced up and down the street. She hoped to spot a deer or a fox so she could send Linnea a picture of her new neighbors.

Hannah had to admit it was pretty out here, even if there was nothing to do. When the wind blew in the right direction, she caught the clean, salty smell of the ocean, and not far from town there were redwood trees so huge her whole family could hold hands and still not wrap their arms all the way around the trunks. And there was a ton of wildlife —so much more than the squirrels and raccoons they had in Michigan. Sometimes Hannah heard coyotes howling at night, and she'd even seen a bald eagle perched in the big fir tree across the street.

But today there was no wildlife in sight, just her

next-door neighbor, Mrs. Gilly, slowly making her way down her driveway.

Mrs. Gilly's walker glinted silver in the sunlight. According to Hannah's mom, she had just had hip surgery, which explained why Hannah hadn't seen her around much. She was a slight woman, older than Hannah's parents. Her gray-streaked hair was knotted in a loose bun. She wore a light khaki vest with lots of small pockets, like a safari guide or a fisherman, and she had a leash looped around one wrist.

At the other end of the leash was a thick-chested, stocky dog with muscular legs. The pup wore a pale pink harness and blue collar. She had a blocky head, short light brown fur with patches of white, and one big spot over her eye and down the side of her face. She practically pranced down the driveway, and when she gazed up at Mrs. Gilly with her tongue hanging out, it looked like she was smiling. As the dog's tail whipped back and forth, she seemed to be the happiest dog in the world.

Hannah had never had a dog of her own and had never really paid much attention to them, but she had to admit that this one was pretty cute. Her smile was simply irresistible, and something about her bright personality reminded Hannah of the California sunshine.

The dog stretched out her front legs and lowered her burly chest to the ground in a playful bow, then leaped up again. Mrs. Gilly's walker had tennis balls attached to the bottom of the front legs to help her glide around easily, but the dog seemed to think they were her toys. She dove for the tennis balls, tipping her head sideways and trying to gnaw on one of them.

"Poppy, no!" Mrs. Gilly cried. "Sit."

The dog sat. But a second later she popped up and pounced on the ball again, nearly yanking Mrs. Gilly and her walker over. Without thinking, Hannah jumped out of her chair and ran across the yard. She snatched up the half-deflated soccer ball Jenny had left in the dry grass and skidded to a stop a few feet from the dog.

"Hey, Poppy!" Hannah sang in a friendly voice. The dog looked her way, the tips of her floppy ears dancing forward. Hannah rolled the soccer ball to her, and the dog pounced on it. Hannah held her breath, hoping Poppy wouldn't pull Mrs. Gilly too hard and make her lose her balance. She didn't want to make things worse.

Poppy wrestled the soccer ball with her front paws, then managed to pick it up between her teeth, even though it was as big as her head. The ball jutted out of her mouth, and she wagged her tail so hard that her whole body wriggled back and forth. She looked at Hannah as if thanking her for the toy. The dog was bursting with such happiness, Hannah couldn't help but laugh out loud.

Don't miss these heartwarming and adventurous tales of rescue dogs in the **AMERICAN DOG** series by **JENNIFER LI SHOTZ**.